MARVEL

A SPIDER-MAN GRAPHIC NOVEL

MILES MORALES
SHOCK WAVES

WRITTEN BY
JUSTIN A. REYNOLDS

ILLUSTRATED BY
PABLO LEON

LAYOUTS BY
GEOFFO

LETTERS BY
VC's ARIANA MAHER

AN IMPRINT OF
SCHOLASTIC

LAUREN BISOM, Editor
CAITLIN O'CONNELL, Associate Editor
ADAM DEL RE, Publication Design
JOE FRONTIRRE with **SALENA MAHINA**, Production
JOE HOCHSTEIN, Associate Manager, Digital Assests
JENNIFER GRÜNWALD, Senior Editor, Special Projects
SVEN LARSEN, VP Licensed Publishing
JEFF YOUNGQUIST, VP Production & Special Projects
DAVID GABRIEL, SVP Print, Sales & Marketing
C.B. CEBULSKI, Editor in Chief

MICHAEL PETRANEK, Executive Editor, Manager AFK & Graphix Media, Scholastic
JESSICA MELTZER, Senior Designer, Scholastic

Spider-Man created by **STAN LEE** & **STEVE DITKO**

With special thanks to **JOHN NEE, JOE QUESADA,
NICK LOWE,** and **RICKEY PURDIN**

ISBN 978-1-338-64803-4

10 9 8 7 6 5 4 3 2 1   21 22 23 24 25

Printed in the U.S.A.   40

First edition, June 2021

Art by Pablo Leon
Letters by Ariana Maher

CHAPTER
ONE

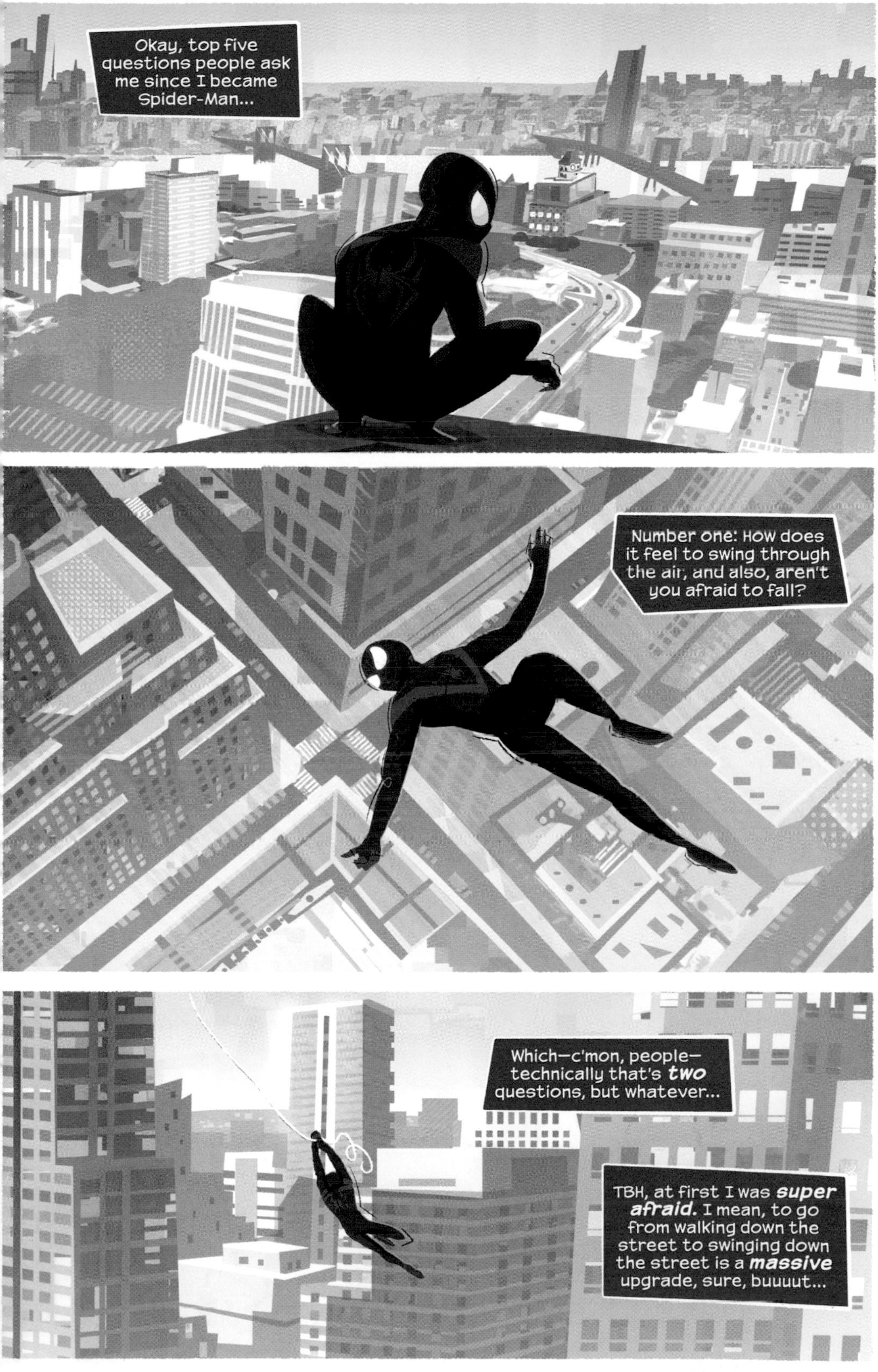
Okay, top five questions people ask me since I became Spider-Man...
Number one: How does it feel to swing through the air, and also, aren't you afraid to fall?
Which—c'mon, people—technically that's **two** questions, but whatever...
TBH, at first I was ***super afraid.*** I mean, to go from walking down the street to swinging down the street is a ***massive*** upgrade, sure, buuuut...

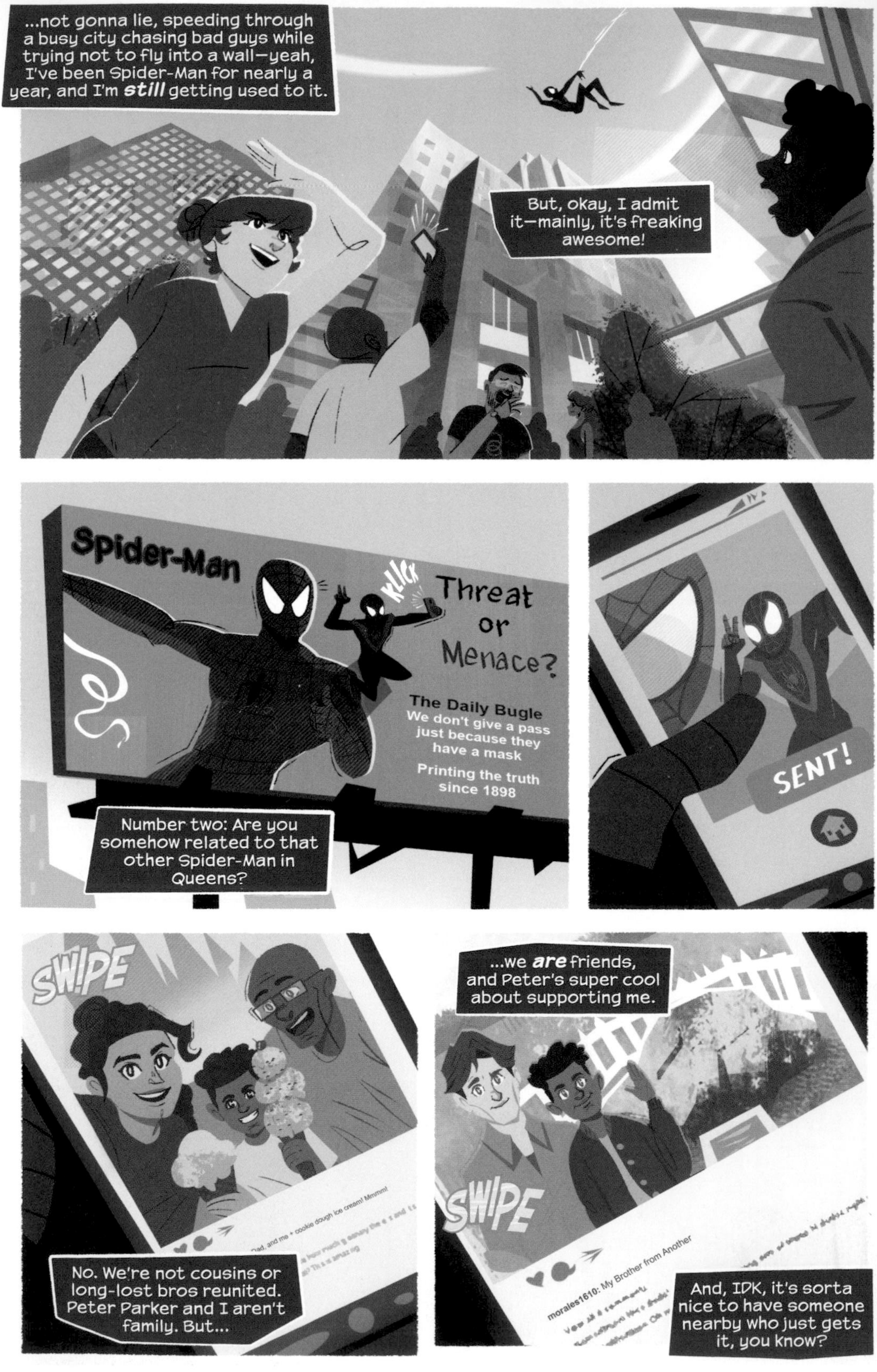

...not gonna lie, speeding through a busy city chasing bad guys while trying not to fly into a wall—yeah, I've been Spider-Man for nearly a year, and I'm ***still*** getting used to it.
But, okay, I admit it—mainly, it's freaking awesome!
Spider-Man
KLICK
Threat or Menace?
The Daily Bugle
We don't give a pass just because they have a mask
Printing the truth since 1898
Number two: Are you somehow related to that other Spider-Man in Queens?
SENT!
SWIPE
Dad, and me + cookie dough ice cream! Mmmm!
No. We're not cousins or long-lost bros reunited. Peter Parker and I aren't family. But...
...we ***are*** friends, and Peter's super cool about supporting me.
SWIPE
morales1610: My Brother from Another
And, IDK, it's sorta nice to have someone nearby who just gets it, you know?

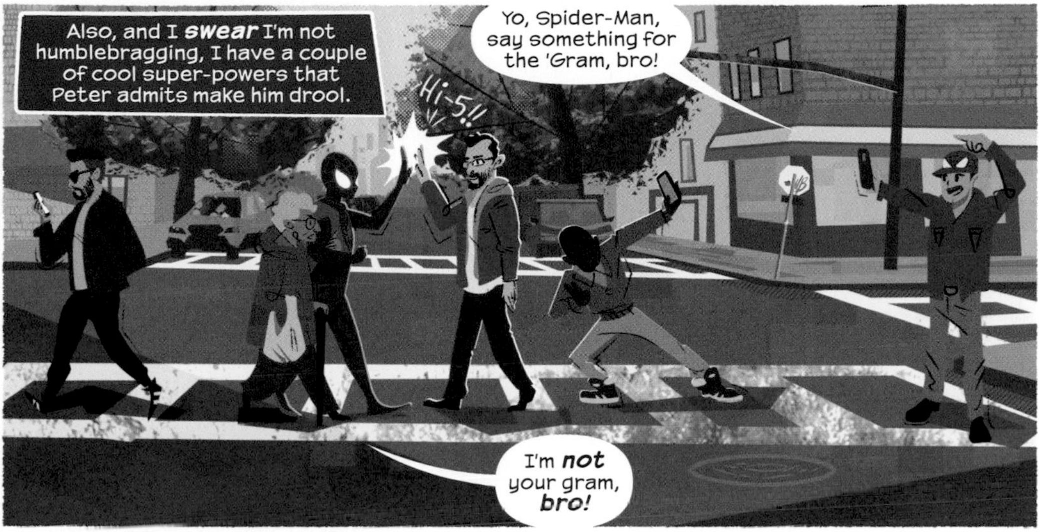
Also, and I **swear** I'm not humblebragging, I have a couple of cool super-powers that Peter admits make him drool.
Yo, Spider-Man, say something for the 'Gram, bro!
Hi-5!!
I'm **not** your gram, **bro!**

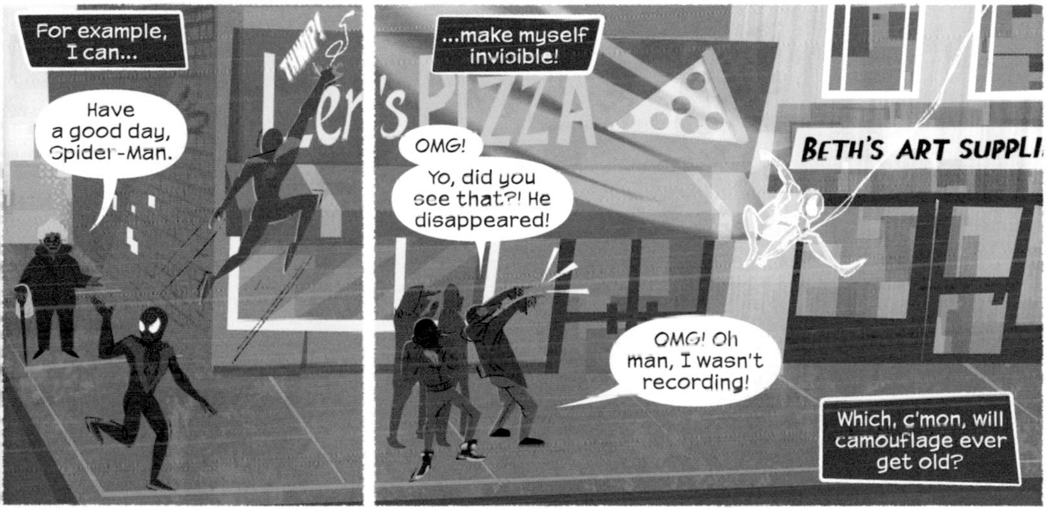
For example, I can...
THWIP!
Have a good day, Spider-Man.
...make myself invisible!
BETH'S ART SUPPLI
OMG!
Yo, did you see that?! He disappeared!
OMG! Oh man, I wasn't recording!
Which, c'mon, will camouflage ever get old?

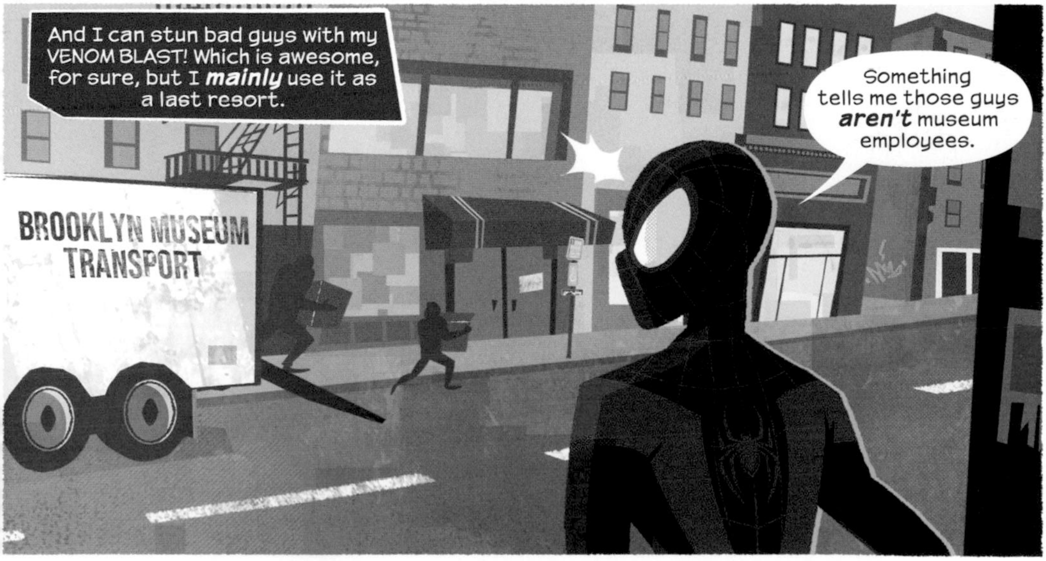
And I can stun bad guys with my VENOM BLAST! Which is awesome, for sure, but I ***mainly*** use it as a last resort.
BROOKLYN MUSEUM TRANSPORT
Something tells me those guys ***aren't*** museum employees.

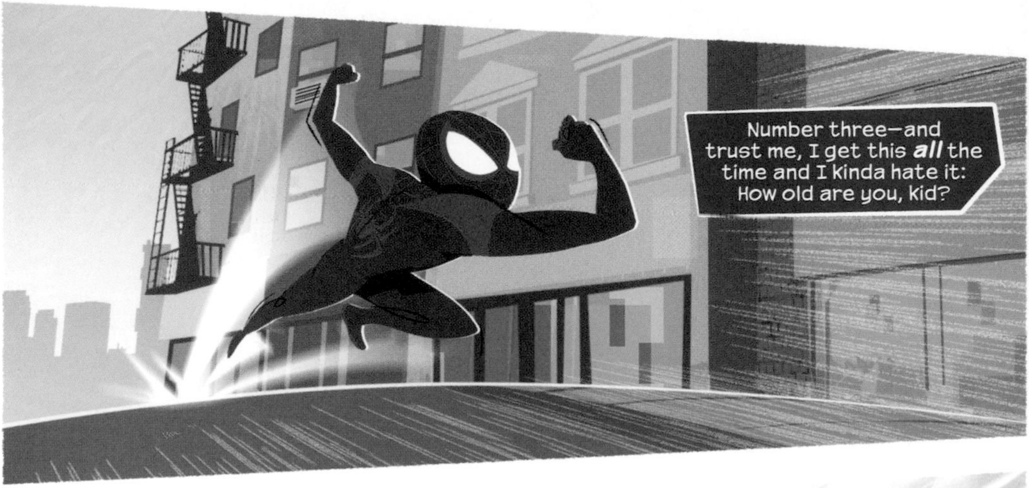
Number three—and trust me, I get this ***all*** the time and I kinda hate it: How old are you, kid?

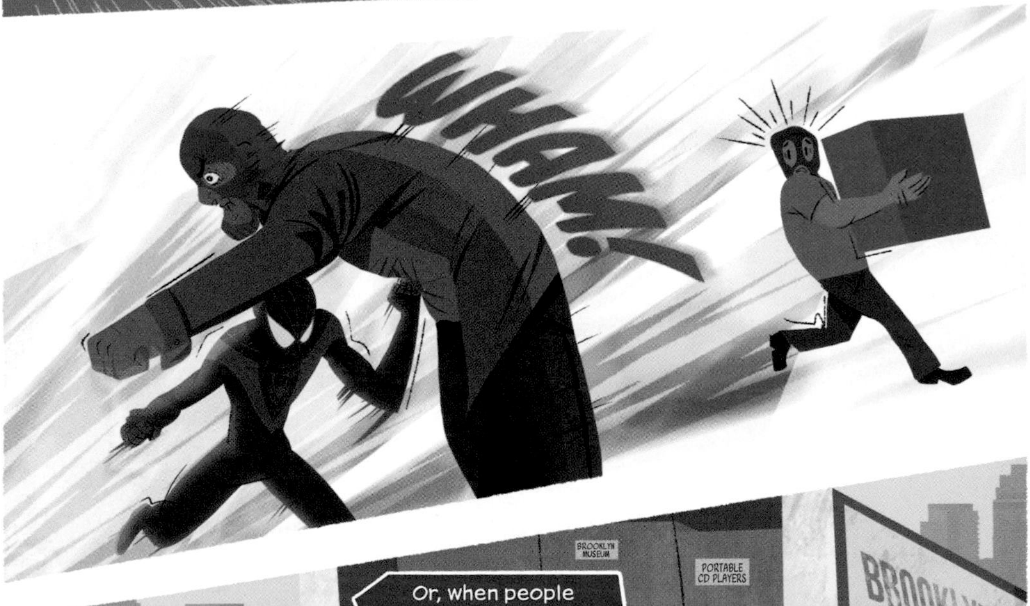
WHAM!

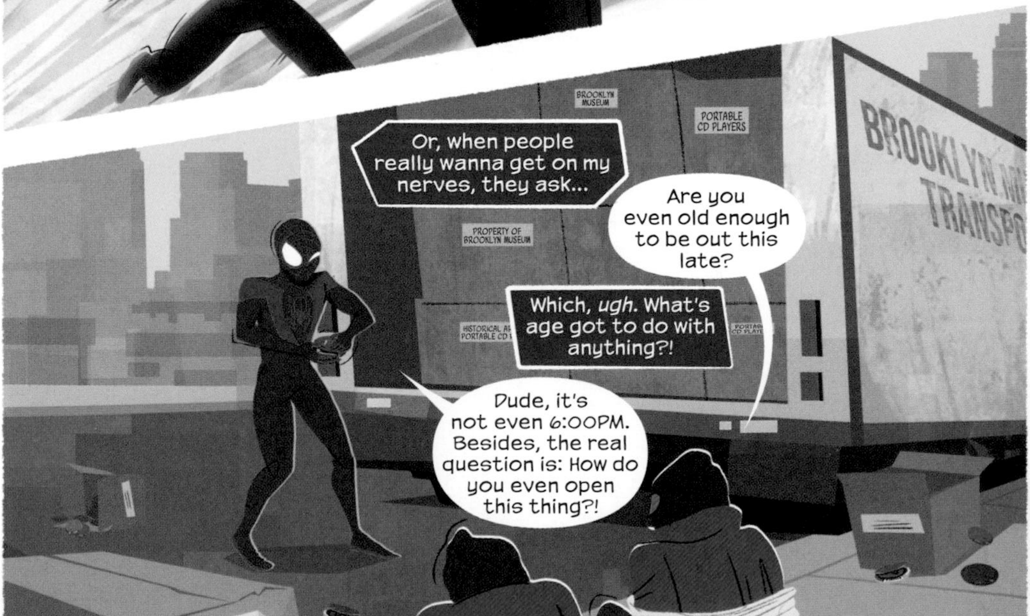
BROOKLYN MUSEUM
PORTABLE CD PLAYERS
Or, when people really wanna get on my nerves, they ask...
Are you even old enough to be out this late?
PROPERTY OF BROOKLYN MUSEUM
Which, *ugh*. What's age got to do with anything?!
Dude, it's not even 6:00PM. Besides, the real question is: How do you even open this thing?!
BROOKLYN MUSEUM HISTORICAL ARCHIVES
PORTABLE CD PLAYERS

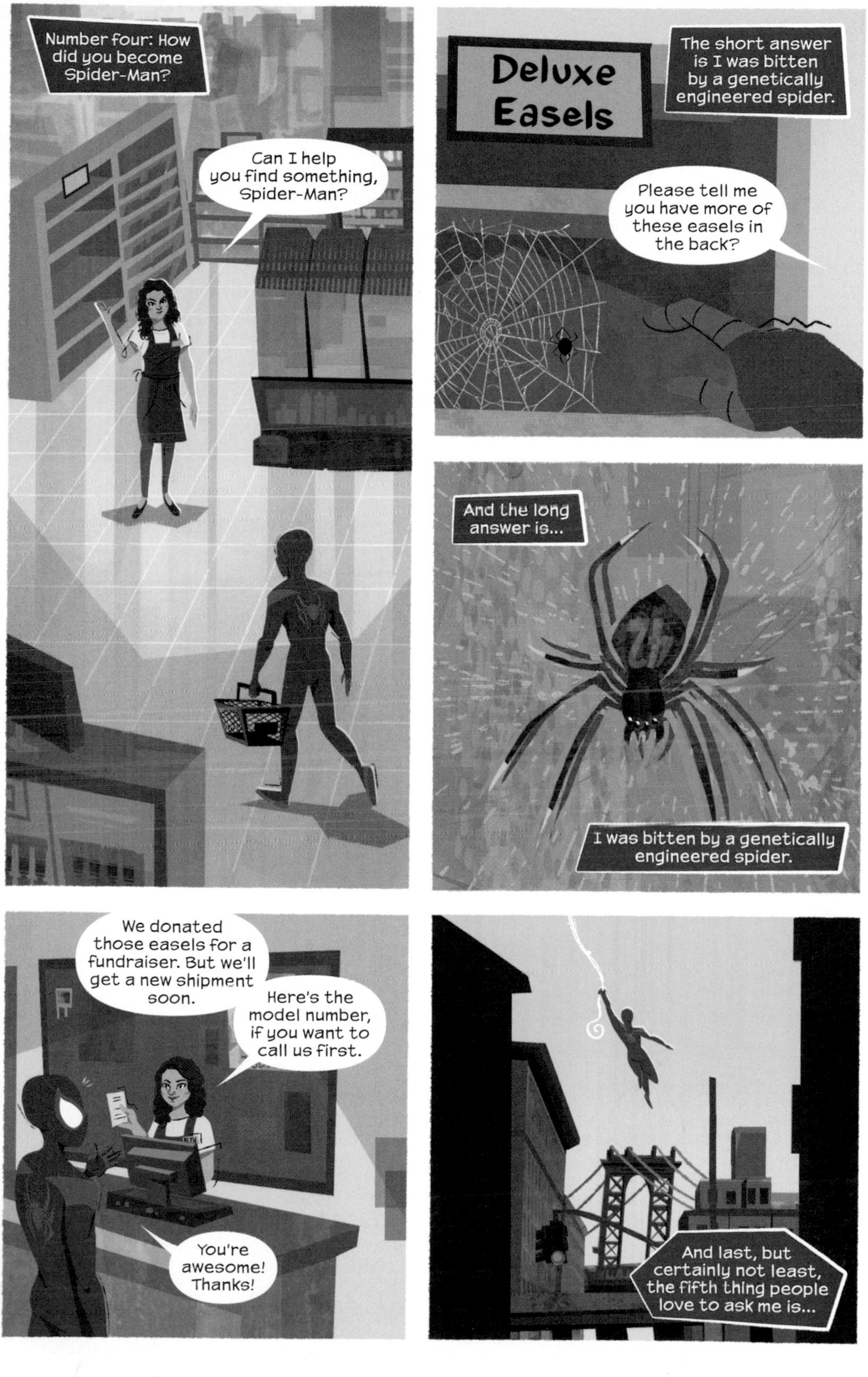

Number four: How did you become Spider-Man?
Can I help you find something, Spider-Man?
Deluxe Easels
The short answer is I was bitten by a genetically engineered spider.
Please tell me you have more of these easels in the back?
And the long answer is...
I was bitten by a genetically engineered spider.
We donated those easels for a fundraiser. But we'll get a new shipment soon.
Here's the model number, if you want to call us first.
You're awesome! Thanks!
And last, but certainly not least, the fifth thing people love to ask me is...

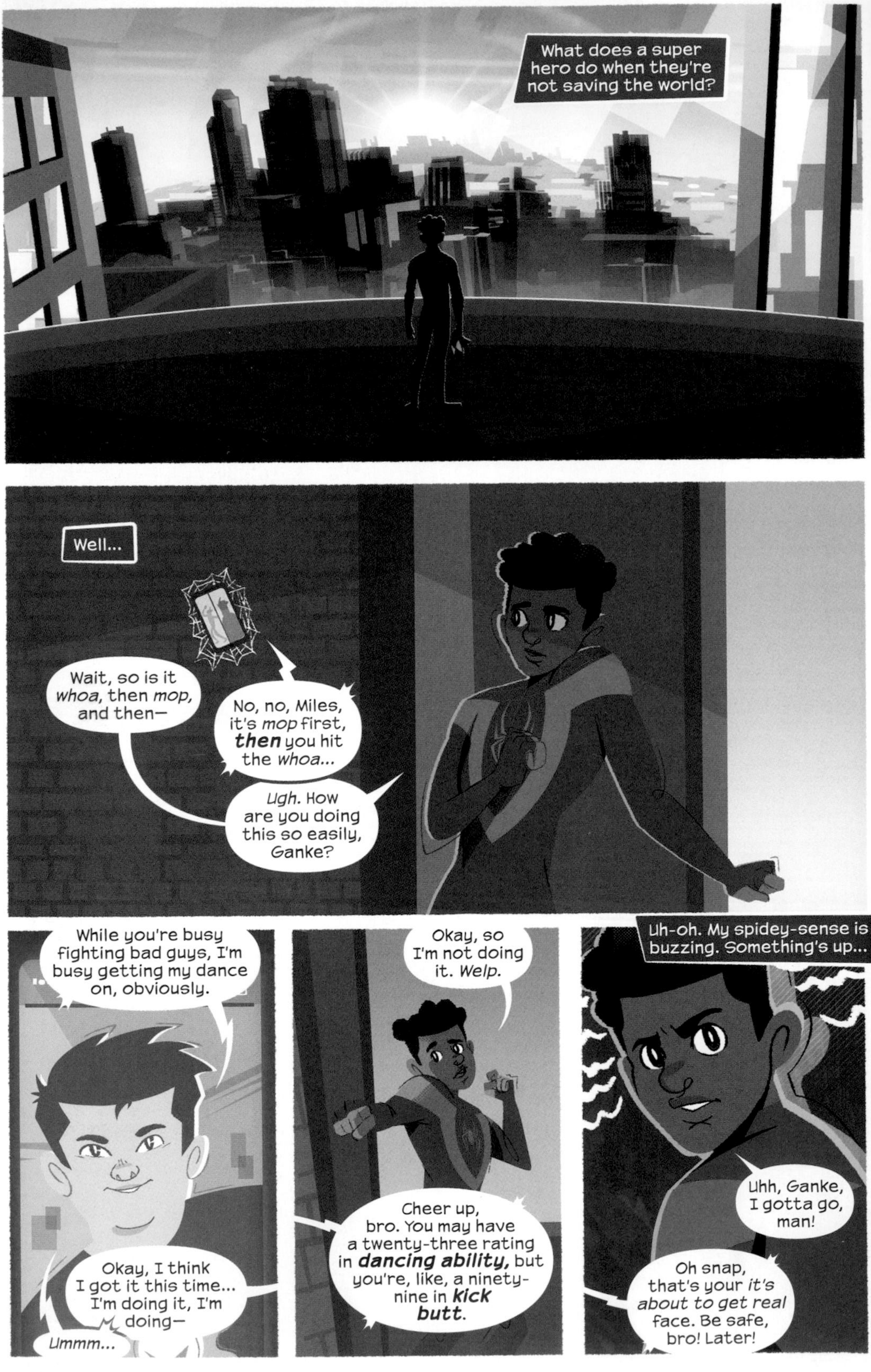

What does a super hero do when they're not saving the world?
Well...
Wait, so is it *whoa*, then *mop*, and then—
No, no, Miles, it's *mop* first, **then** you hit the *whoa*...
Ugh. How are you doing this so easily, Ganke?
While you're busy fighting bad guys, I'm busy getting my dance on, obviously.
Okay, I think I got it this time... I'm doing it, I'm doing—
Ummm...
Okay, so I'm not doing it. *Welp.*
Cheer up, bro. You may have a twenty-three rating in ***dancing ability,*** but you're, like, a ninety-nine in ***kick butt***.
Uh-oh. My spidey-sense is buzzing. Something's up...
Uhh, Ganke, I gotta go, man!
Oh snap, that's your *it's about to get real* face. Be safe, bro! Later!

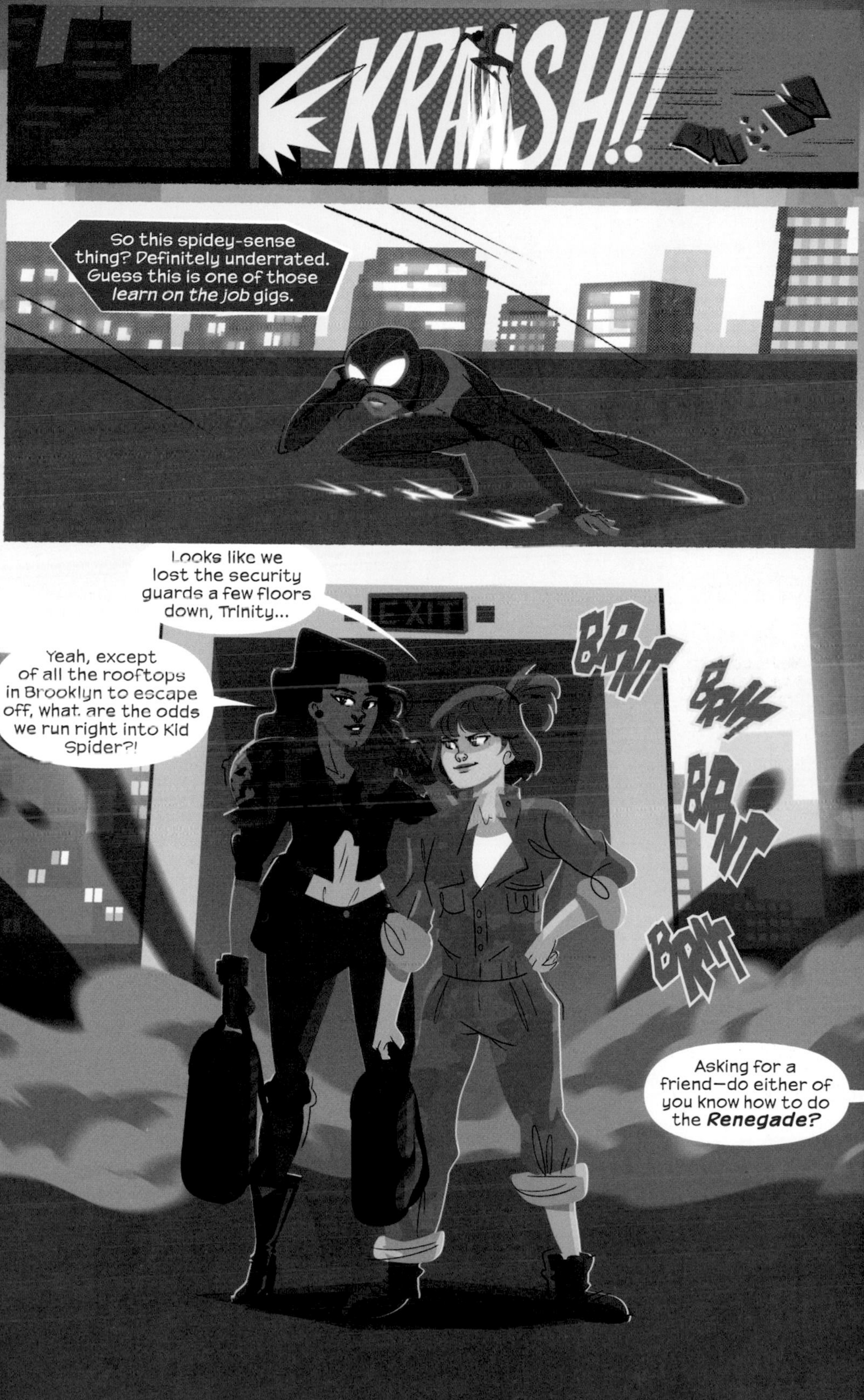
KRAASH!!
So this spidey-sense thing? Definitely underrated. Guess this is one of those *learn on the job* gigs.
Looks like we lost the security guards a few floors down, Trinity...
EXIT
Yeah, except of all the rooftops in Brooklyn to escape off, what are the odds we run right into Kid Spider?!
BRNT
BRNT
BRNT
BRNT
Asking for a friend—do either of you know how to do the ***Renegade?***

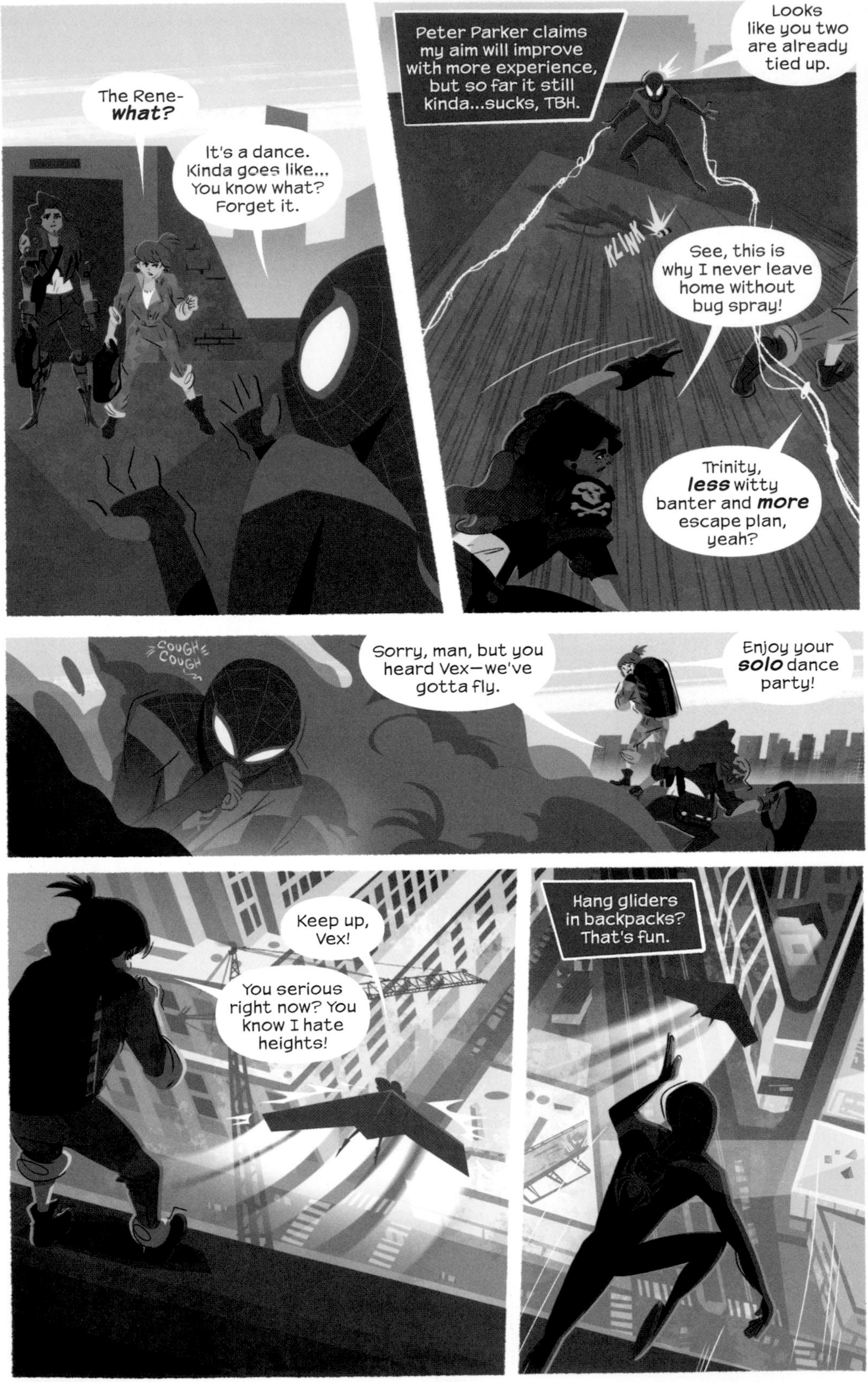

The Rene-
what?
It's a dance. Kinda goes like... You know what? Forget it.
Peter Parker claims my aim will improve with more experience, but so far it still kinda...sucks, TBH.
Looks like you two are already tied up.
KLINK
See, this is why I never leave home without bug spray!
Trinity, **less** witty banter and **more** escape plan, yeah?
COUGH COUGH
Sorry, man, but you heard Vex—we've gotta fly.
Enjoy your **solo** dance party!
Keep up, Vex!
You serious right now? You know I hate heights!
Hang gliders in backpacks? That's fun.

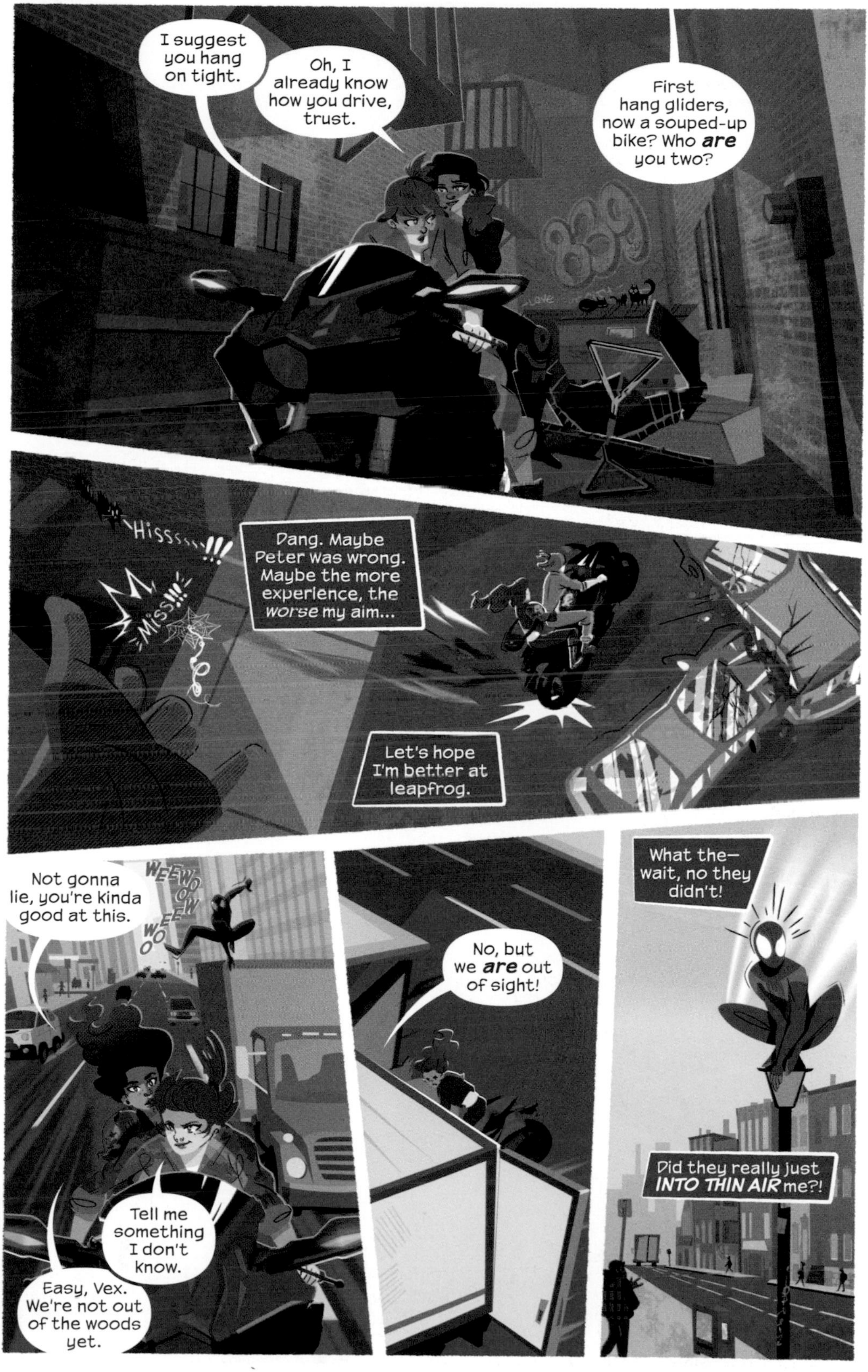
I suggest you hang on tight.
Oh, I already know how you drive, trust.
First hang gliders, now a souped-up bike? Who *are* you two?
Hisssss...!!!
Miss!!!
Dang. Maybe Peter was wrong. Maybe the more experience, the *worse* my aim...
Let's hope I'm better at leapfrog.
Not gonna lie, you're kinda good at this.
WEEWOO WEEWOO
Tell me something I don't know.
Easy, Vex. We're not out of the woods yet.
No, but we *are* out of sight!
What the—wait, no they didn't!
Did they really just ***INTO THIN AIR*** me?!

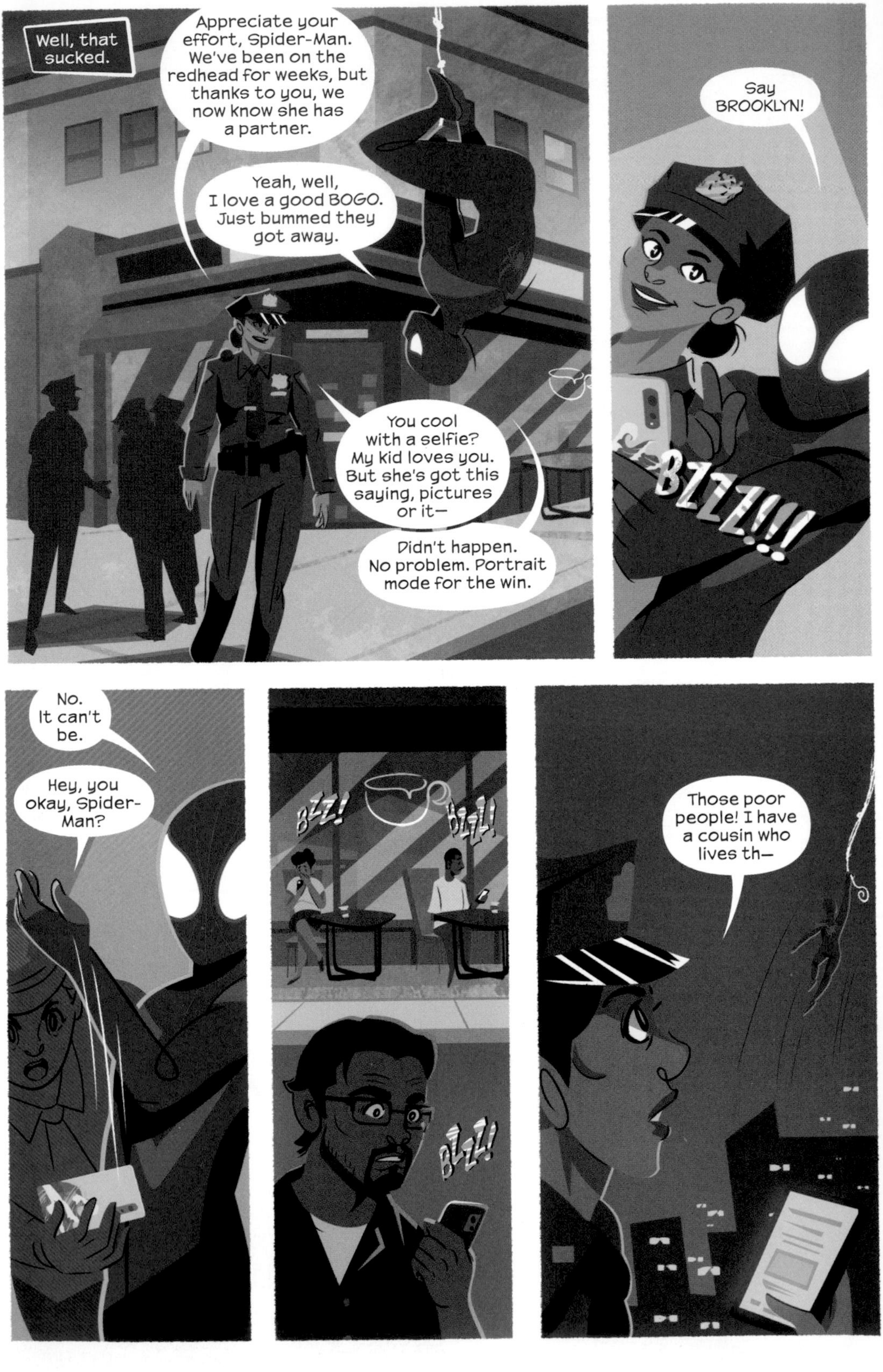

Well, that sucked.
Appreciate your effort, Spider-Man. We've been on the redhead for weeks, but thanks to you, we now know she has a partner.
Yeah, well, I love a good BOGO. Just bummed they got away.
You cool with a selfie? My kid loves you. But she's got this saying, pictures or it—
Didn't happen. No problem. Portrait mode for the win.
Say BROOKLYN!
BZZZ!!!
No. It can't be.
Hey, you okay, Spider-Man?
BZZ!
BZZ!
BZZ!
Those poor people! I have a cousin who lives th—

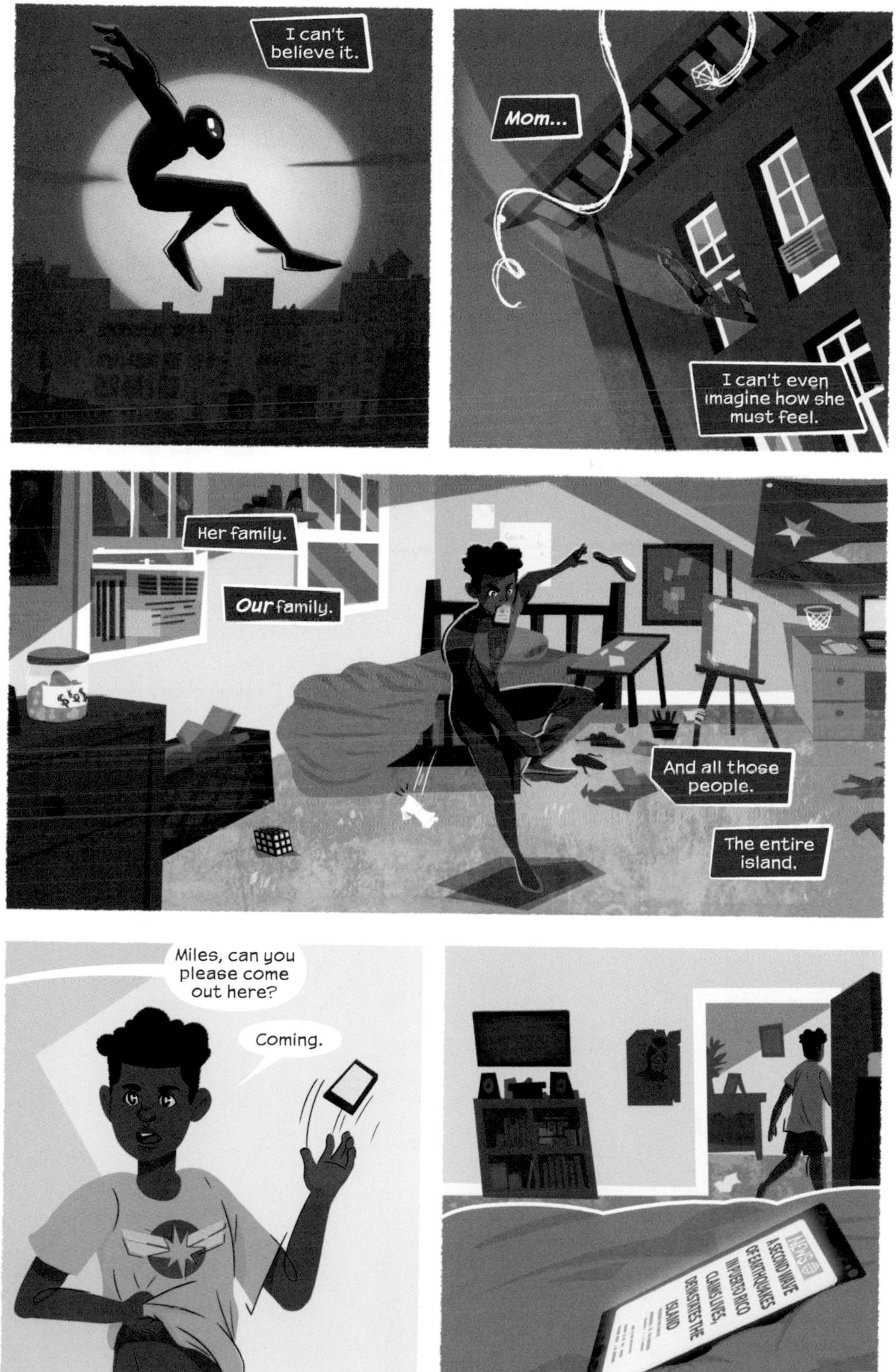
I can't believe it.
Mom...
I can't even imagine how she must feel.
Her family.
Our family.
And all those people.
The entire island.
Miles, can you please come out here?
Coming.
NEWS
A SECOND WAVE OF EARTHQUAKES IN PUERTO RICO CLAIMS LIVES, DEVASTATES THE ISLAND

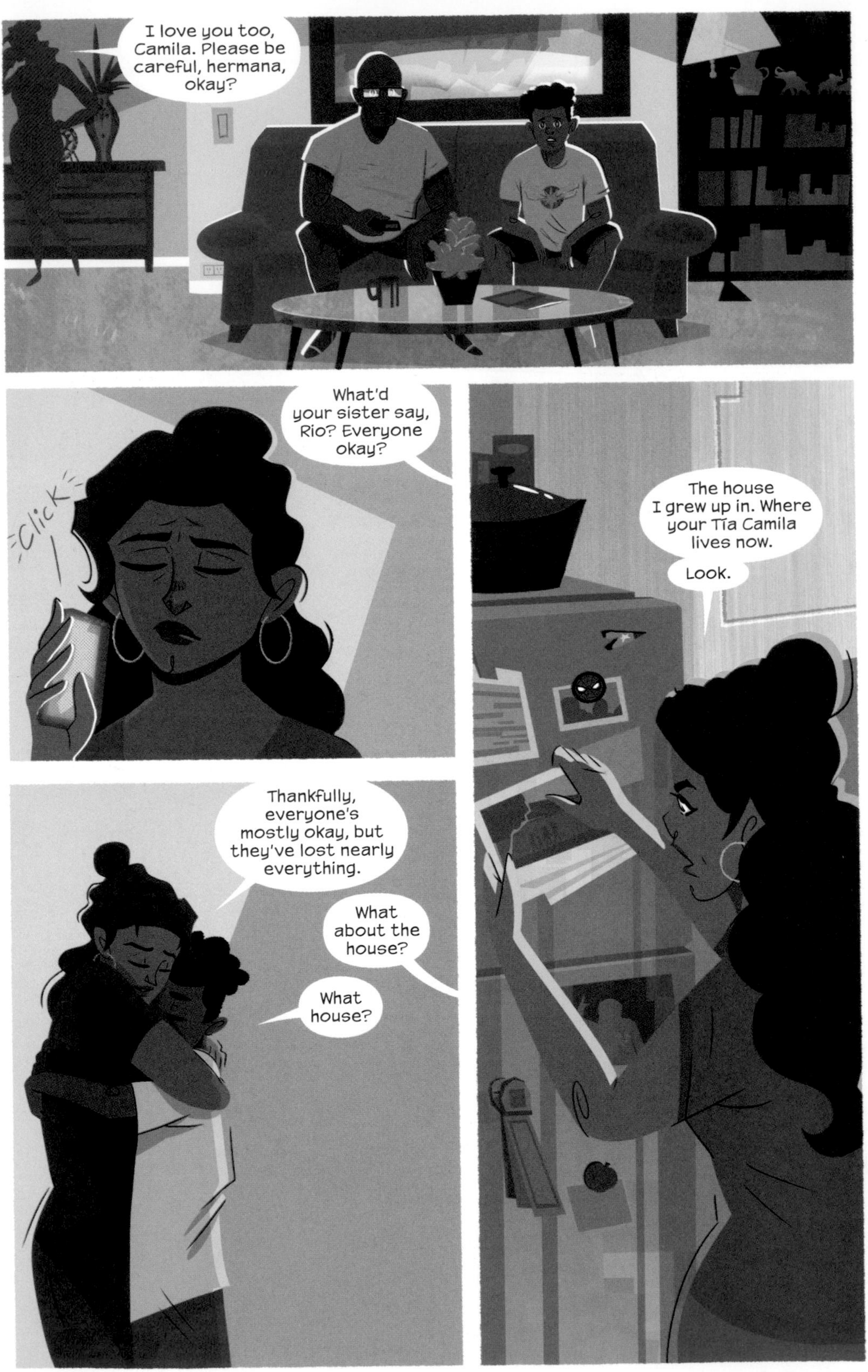
I love you too, Camila. Please be careful, hermana, okay?
What'd your sister say, Rio? Everyone okay?
CLICK
Thankfully, everyone's mostly okay, but they've lost nearly everything.
What about the house?
What house?
The house I grew up in. Where your Tía Camila lives now.
Look.

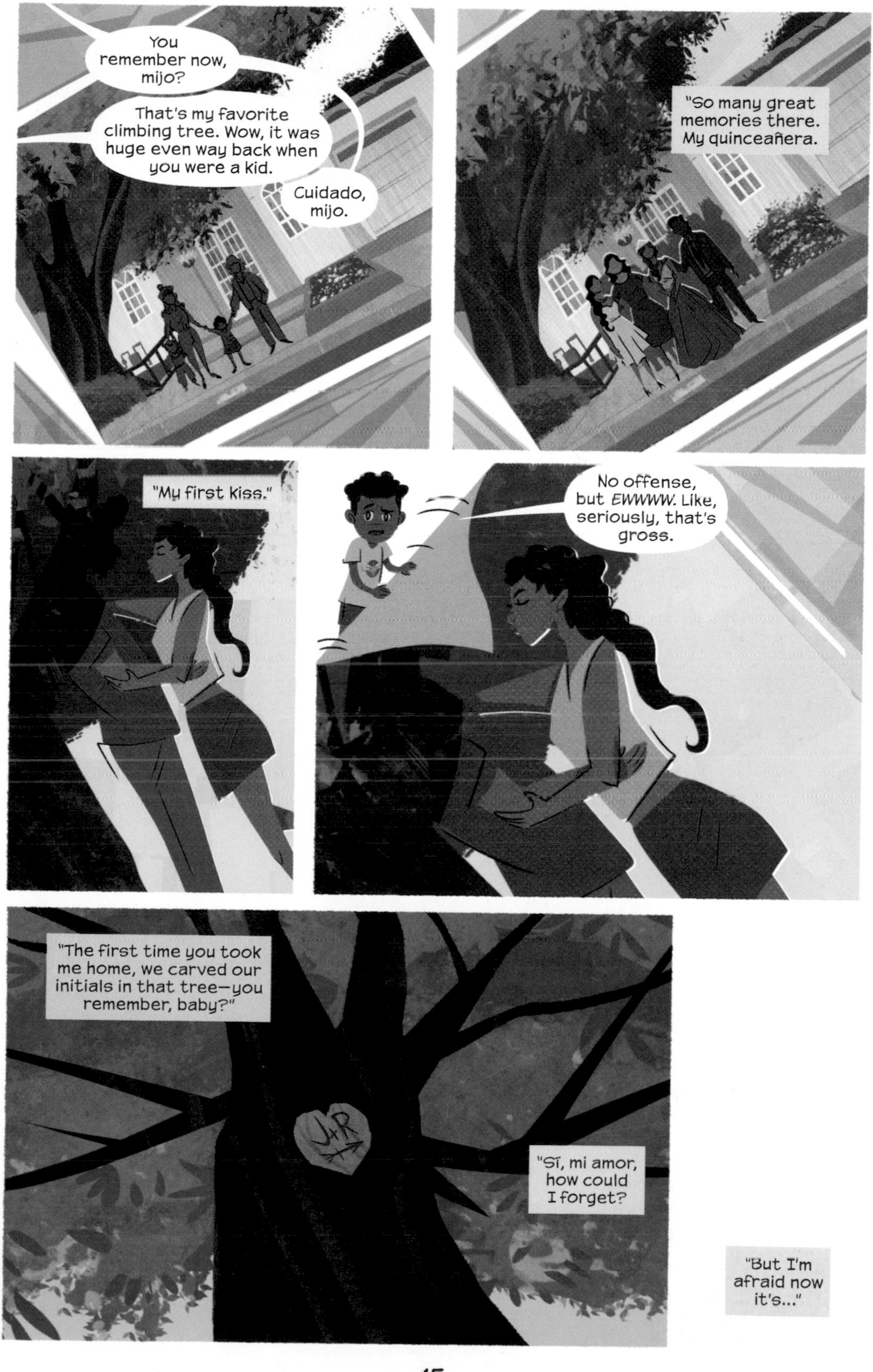
You remember now, mijo?
That's my favorite climbing tree. Wow, it was huge even way back when you were a kid.
Cuidado, mijo.
"So many great memories there. My quinceañera.
"My first kiss."
No offense, but EWWWW. Like, seriously, that's gross.
"The first time you took me home, we carved our initials in that tree—you remember, baby?"
J+R
"Sí, mi amor, how could I forget?
"But I'm afraid now it's..."

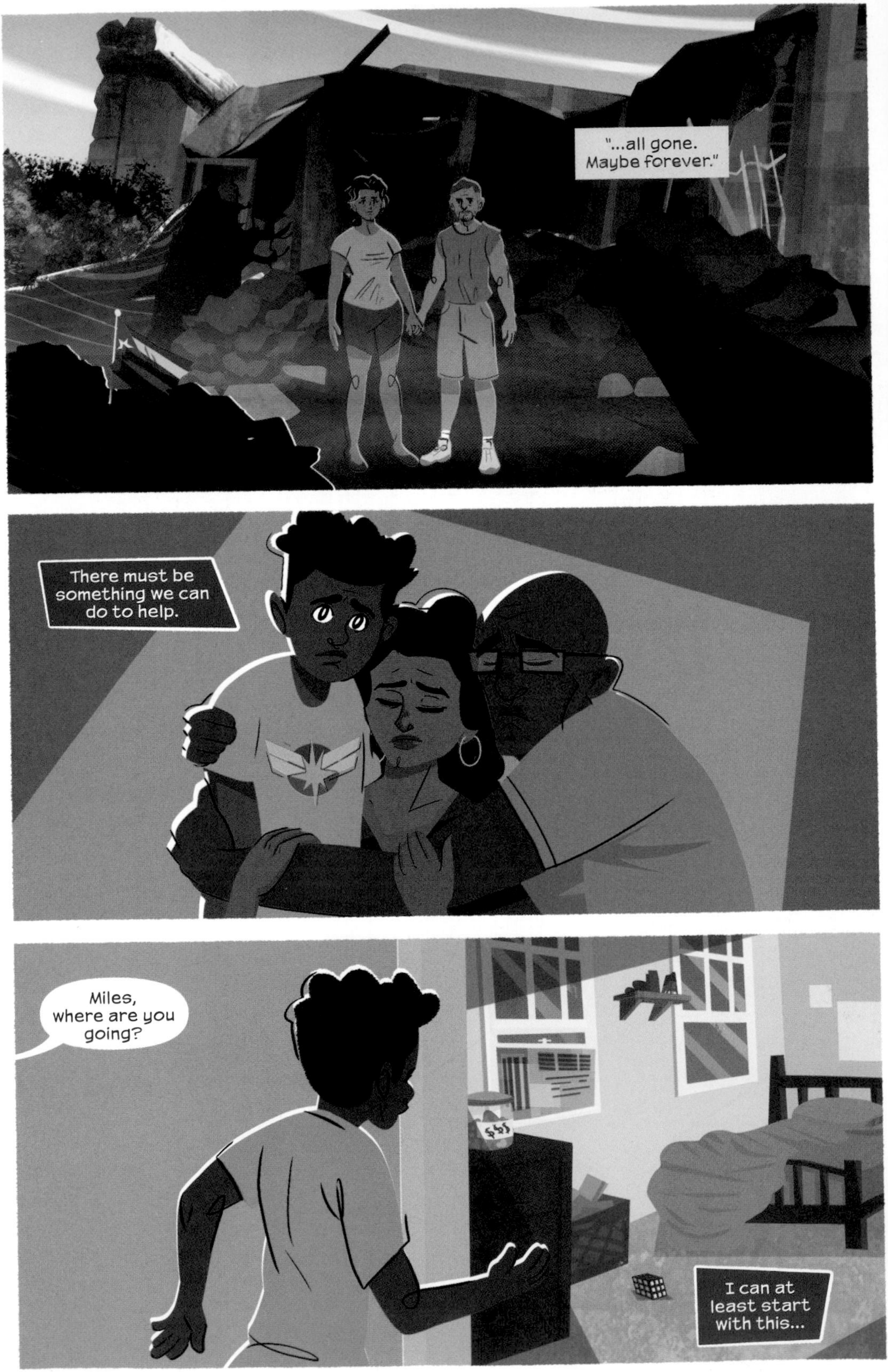
"...all gone. Maybe forever."
There must be something we can do to help.
Miles, where are you going?
I can at least start with this...
$$$

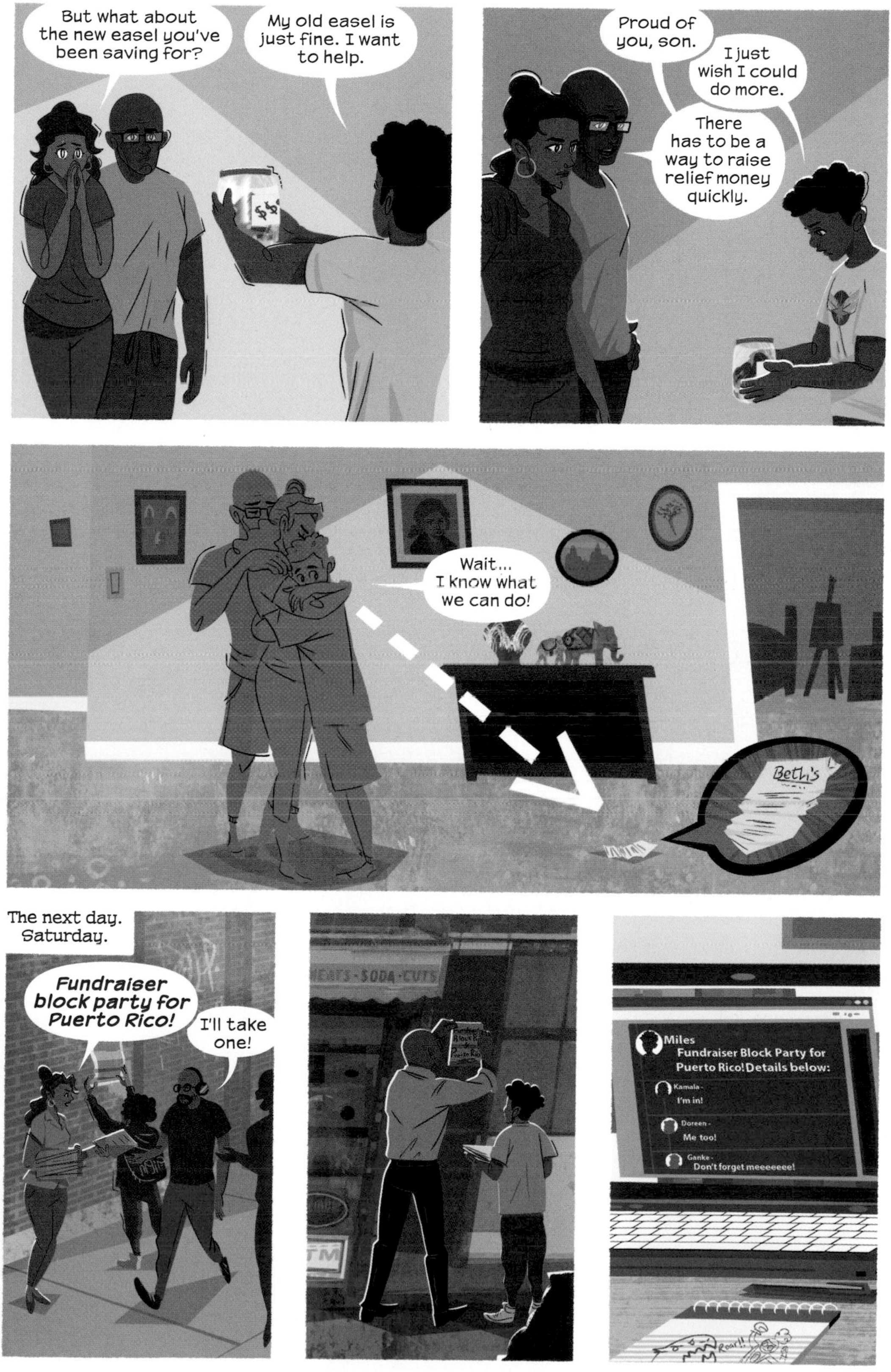

But what about the new easel you've been saving for?
My old easel is just fine. I want to help.
Proud of you, son.
I just wish I could do more.
There has to be a way to raise relief money quickly.
Wait... I know what we can do!
Beth's
The next day. Saturday.
Fundraiser block party for Puerto Rico!
I'll take one!
Miles
Fundraiser Block Party for Puerto Rico! Details below:
Kamala -
I'm in!
Doreen -
Me too!
Ganke -
Don't forget meeeeeee!
Roar!!

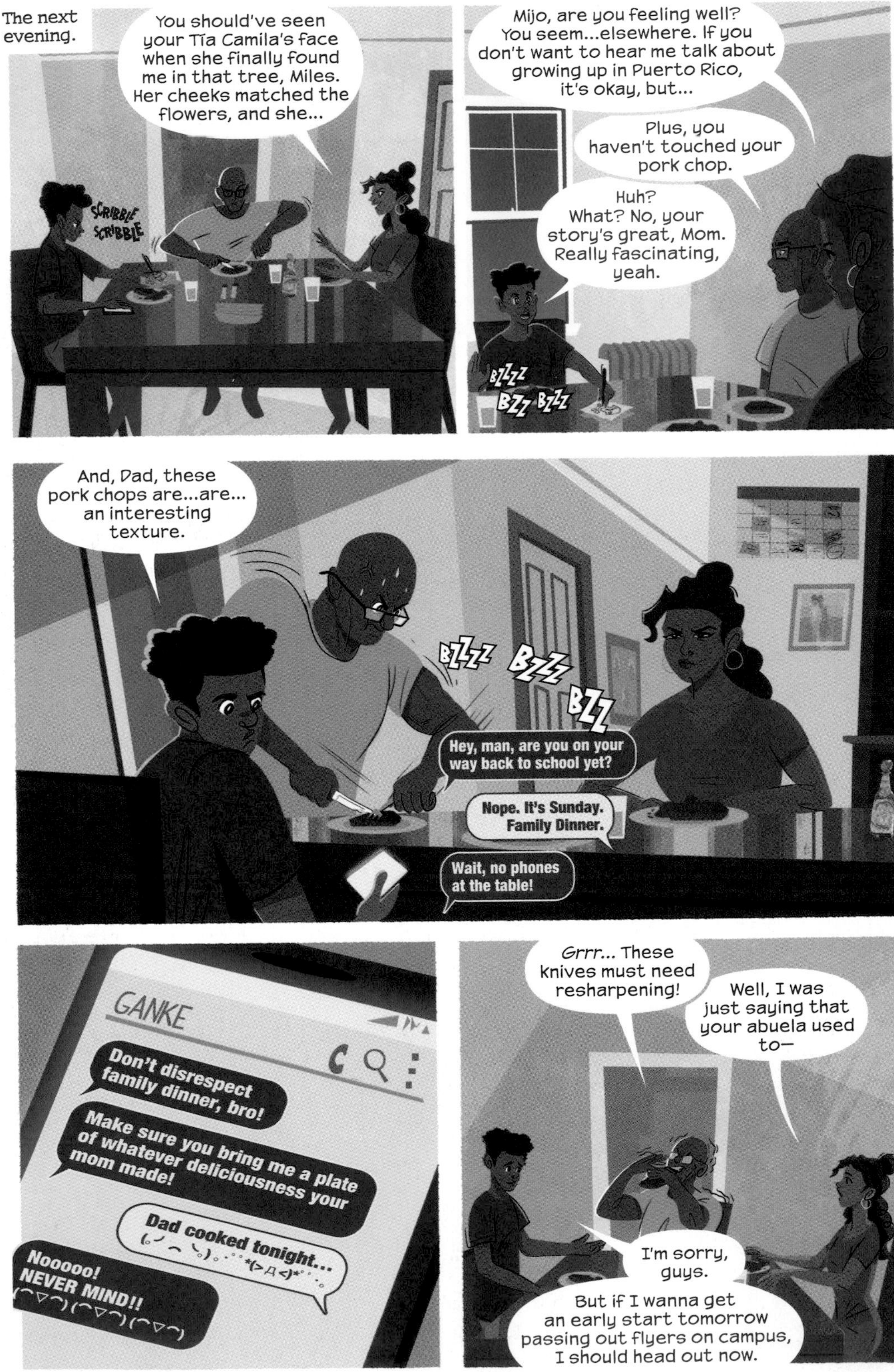
The next evening.
You should've seen your Tía Camila's face when she finally found me in that tree, Miles. Her cheeks matched the flowers, and she...
SCRIBBLE SCRIBBLE
Mijo, are you feeling well? You seem...elsewhere. If you don't want to hear me talk about growing up in Puerto Rico, it's okay, but...
Plus, you haven't touched your pork chop.
Huh? What? No, your story's great, Mom. Really fascinating, yeah.
BZZZZ BZZ BZZZ
And, Dad, these pork chops are...are... an interesting texture.
BZZZZ BZZZ BZZ
Hey, man, are you on your way back to school yet?
Nope. It's Sunday. Family Dinner.
Wait, no phones at the table!
GANKE
Don't disrespect family dinner, bro!
Make sure you bring me a plate of whatever deliciousness your mom made!
Dad cooked tonight... (｡╯︵╰｡)｡˚°*(>Д<)*°˚｡
Nooooo! NEVER MIND!! (⌒▽⌒)(⌒▽⌒)(⌒▽⌒)
Grrr... These knives must need resharpening!
Well, I was just saying that your abuela used to—
I'm sorry, guys.
But if I wanna get an early start tomorrow passing out flyers on campus, I should head out now.

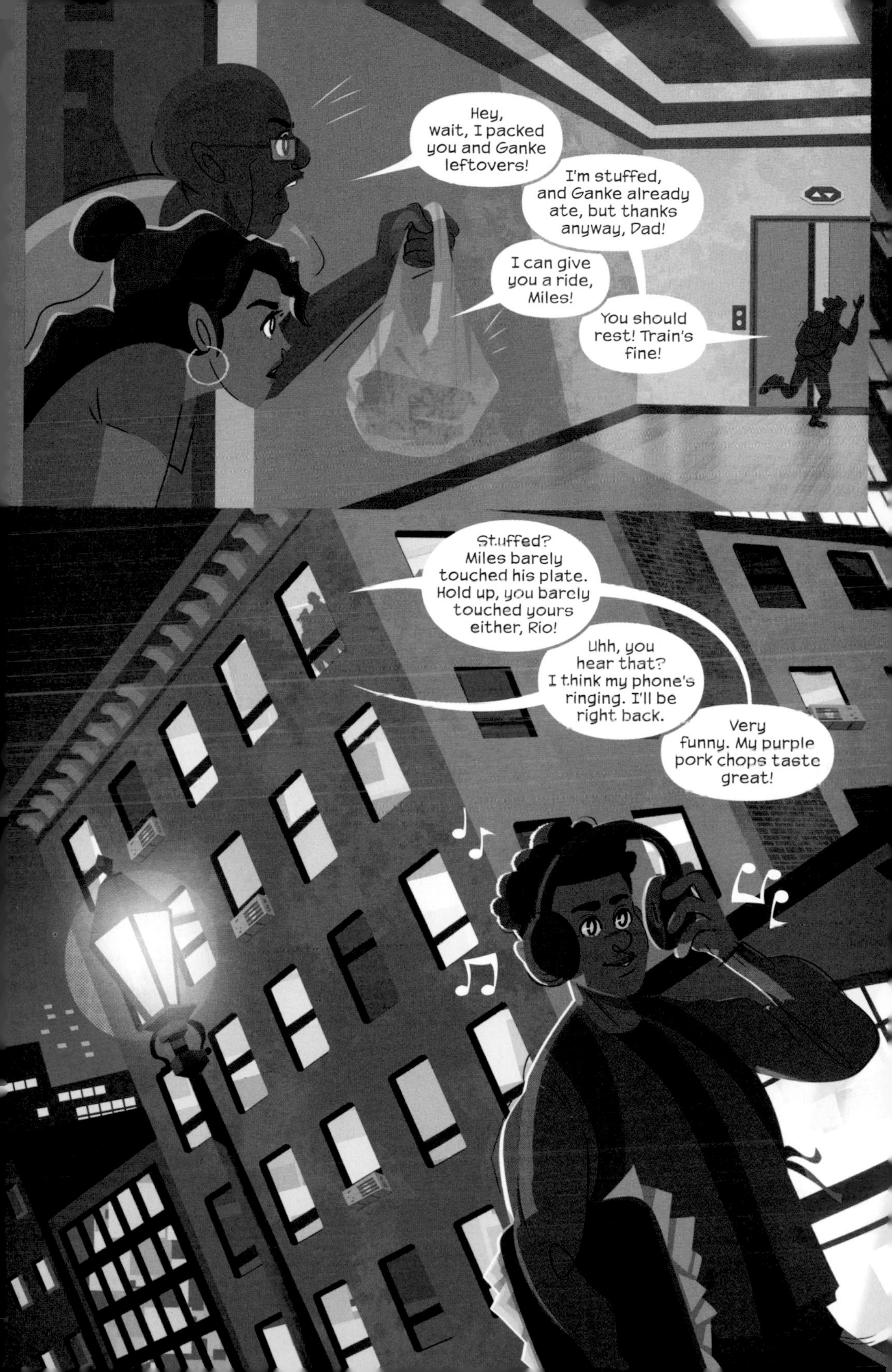
Hey, wait, I packed you and Ganke leftovers!
I'm stuffed, and Ganke already ate, but thanks anyway, Dad!
I can give you a ride, Miles!
You should rest! Train's fine!
Stuffed? Miles barely touched his plate. Hold up, you barely touched yours either, Rio!
Uhh, you hear that? I think my phone's ringing. I'll be right back.
Very funny. My purple pork chops taste great!

CHAPTER

TWO

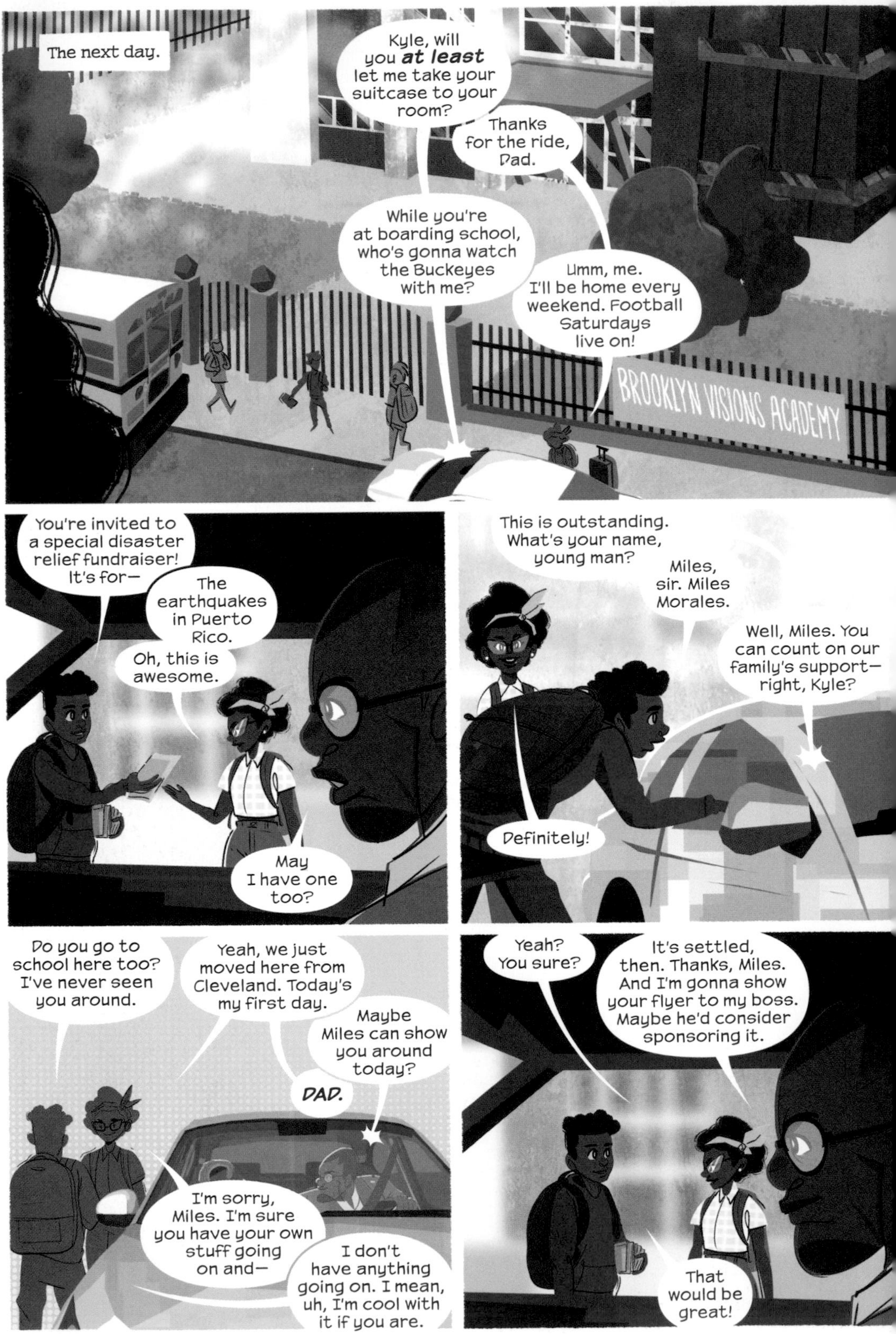

The next day.
Kyle, will you ***at least*** let me take your suitcase to your room?
Thanks for the ride, Dad.
While you're at boarding school, who's gonna watch the Buckeyes with me?
Umm, me. I'll be home every weekend. Football Saturdays live on!
BROOKLYN VISIONS ACADEMY
You're invited to a special disaster relief fundraiser! It's for—
The earthquakes in Puerto Rico.
Oh, this is awesome.
May I have one too?
This is outstanding. What's your name, young man?
Miles, sir. Miles Morales.
Well, Miles. You can count on our family's support—right, Kyle?
Definitely!
Do you go to school here too? I've never seen you around.
Yeah, we just moved here from Cleveland. Today's my first day.
Maybe Miles can show you around today?
DAD.
I'm sorry, Miles. I'm sure you have your own stuff going on and—
I don't have anything going on. I mean, uh, I'm cool with it if you are.
Yeah? You sure?
It's settled, then. Thanks, Miles. And I'm gonna show your flyer to my boss. Maybe he'd consider sponsoring it.
That would be great!

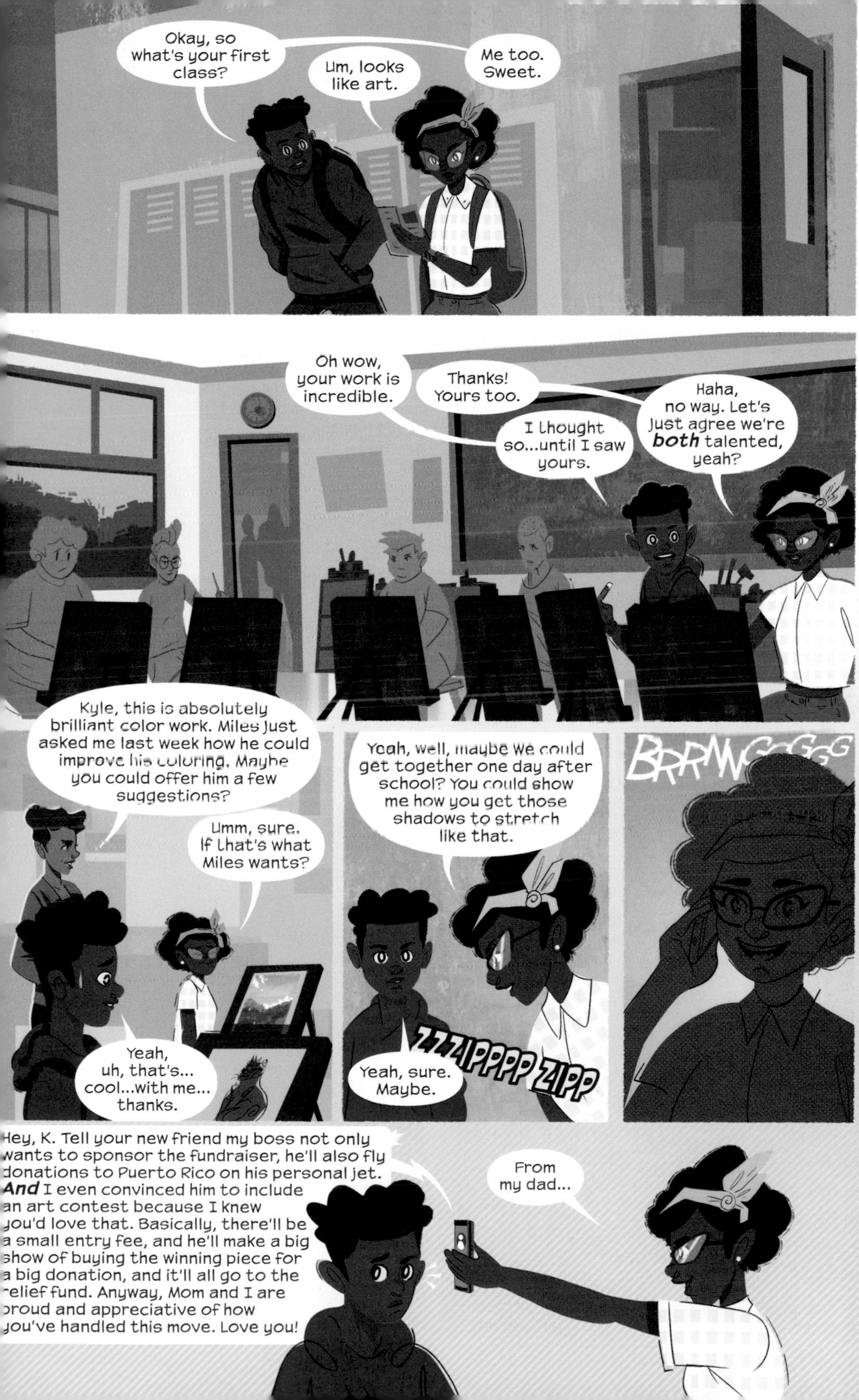

Okay, so what's your first class?
Um, looks like art.
Me too. Sweet.
Oh wow, your work is incredible.
Thanks! Yours too.
I thought so...until I saw yours.
Haha, no way. Let's just agree we're ***both*** talented, yeah?
Kyle, this is absolutely brilliant color work. Miles just asked me last week how he could improve his coloring. Maybe you could offer him a few suggestions?
Umm, sure. If that's what Miles wants?
Yeah, uh, that's... cool...with me... thanks.
Yeah, well, maybe we could get together one day after school? You could show me how you get those shadows to stretch like that.
Yeah, sure. Maybe.
ZZZIPPPP ZIPP
BRRNGGGG
Hey, K. Tell your new friend my boss not only wants to sponsor the fundraiser, he'll also fly donations to Puerto Rico on his personal jet. ***And*** I even convinced him to include an art contest because I knew you'd love that. Basically, there'll be a small entry fee, and he'll make a big show of buying the winning piece for a big donation, and it'll all go to the relief fund. Anyway, Mom and I are proud and appreciative of how you've handled this move. Love you!
From my dad...

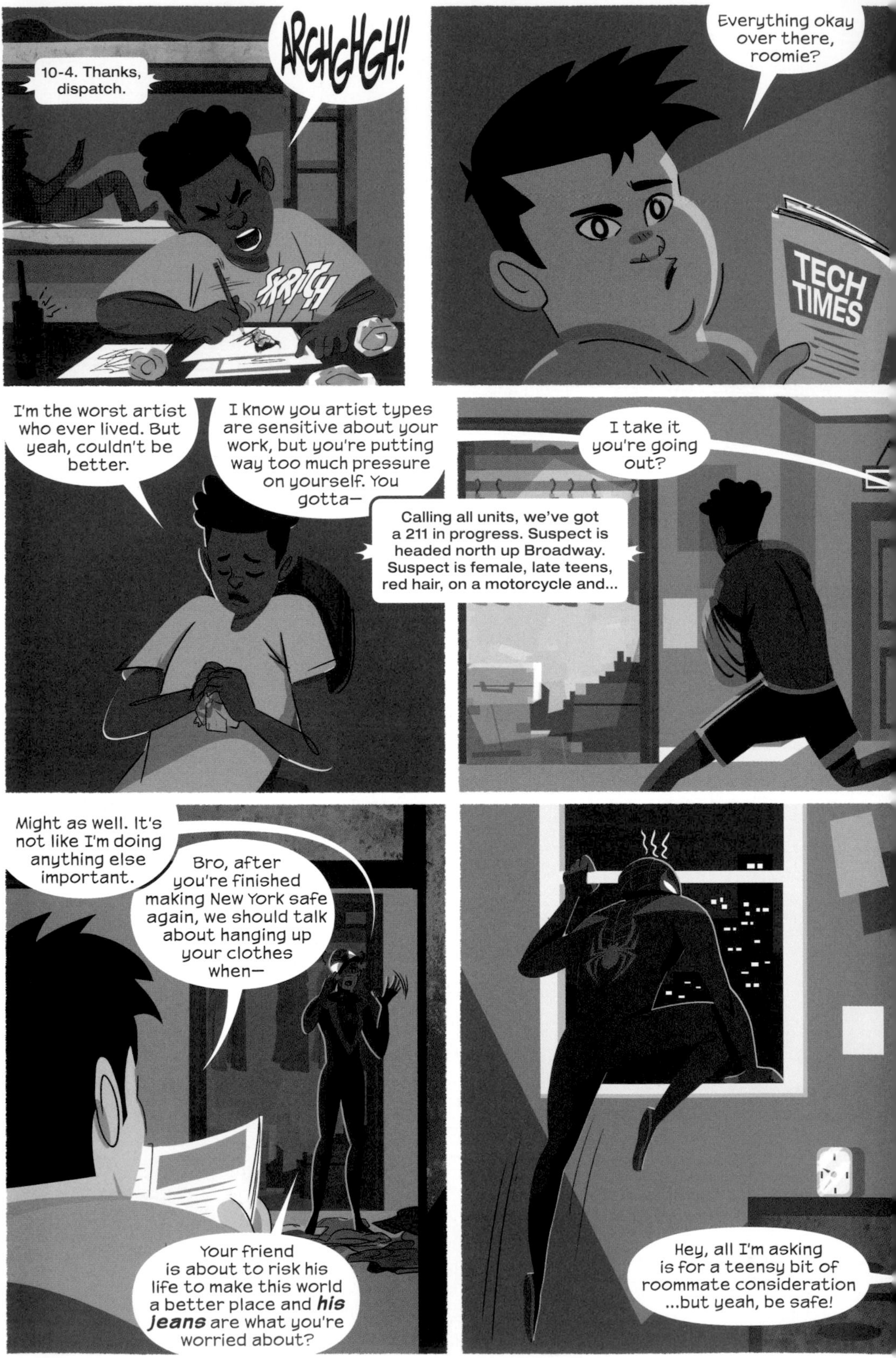
10-4. Thanks, dispatch.
ARGHGHGH!
SKRITCH
Everything okay over there, roomie?
TECH TIMES
I'm the worst artist who ever lived. But yeah, couldn't be better.
I know you artist types are sensitive about your work, but you're putting way too much pressure on yourself. You gotta—
Calling all units, we've got a 211 in progress. Suspect is headed north up Broadway. Suspect is female, late teens, red hair, on a motorcycle and...
I take it you're going out?
Might as well. It's not like I'm doing anything else important.
Bro, after you're finished making New York safe again, we should talk about hanging up your clothes when—
Your friend is about to risk his life to make this world a better place and ***his jeans*** are what you're worried about?
Hey, all I'm asking is for a teensy bit of roommate consideration ...but yeah, be safe!

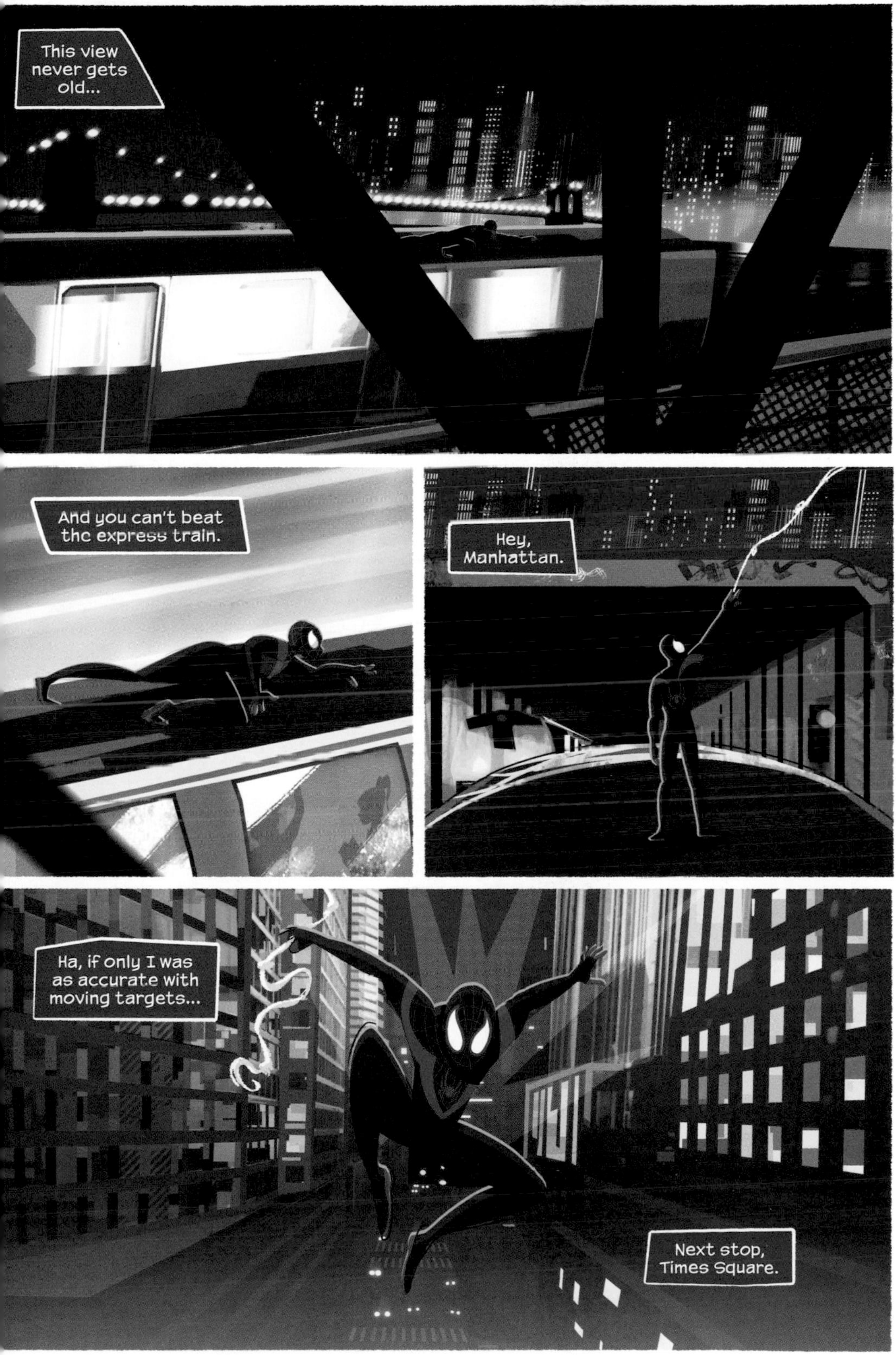
This view never gets old...
And you can't beat the express train.
Hey, Manhattan.
Ha, if only I was as accurate with moving targets...
Next stop, Times Square.

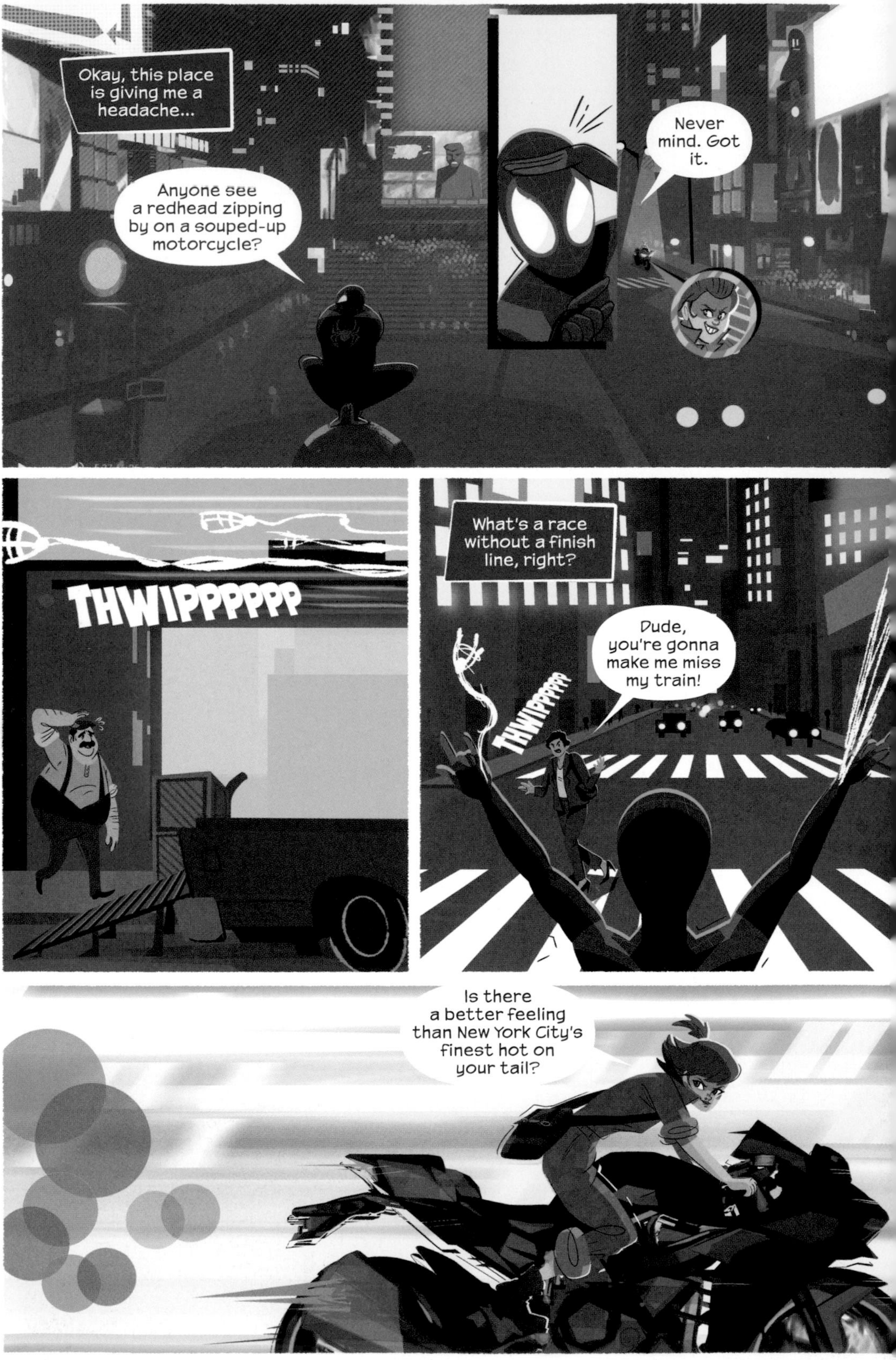

Okay, this place is giving me a headache...
Anyone see a redhead zipping by on a souped-up motorcycle?
Never mind. Got it.
THWIPPPPPP
What's a race without a finish line, right?
Dude, you're gonna make me miss my train!
THWIPPPPP
Is there a better feeling than New York City's finest hot on your tail?

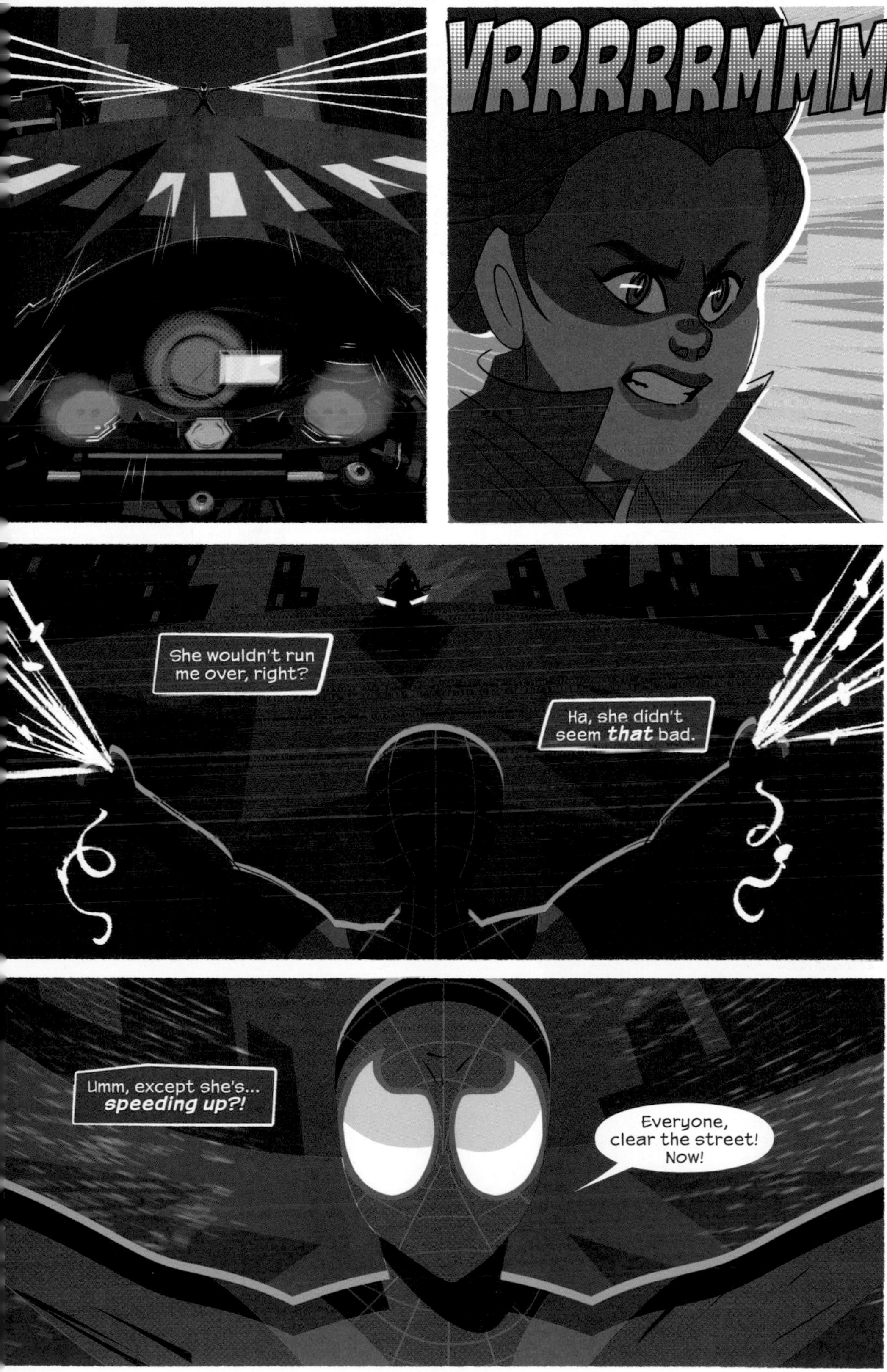
VRRRRRMMMM
She wouldn't run me over, right?
Ha, she didn't seem *that* bad.
Umm, except she's... ***speeding up?!***
Everyone, clear the street! Now!

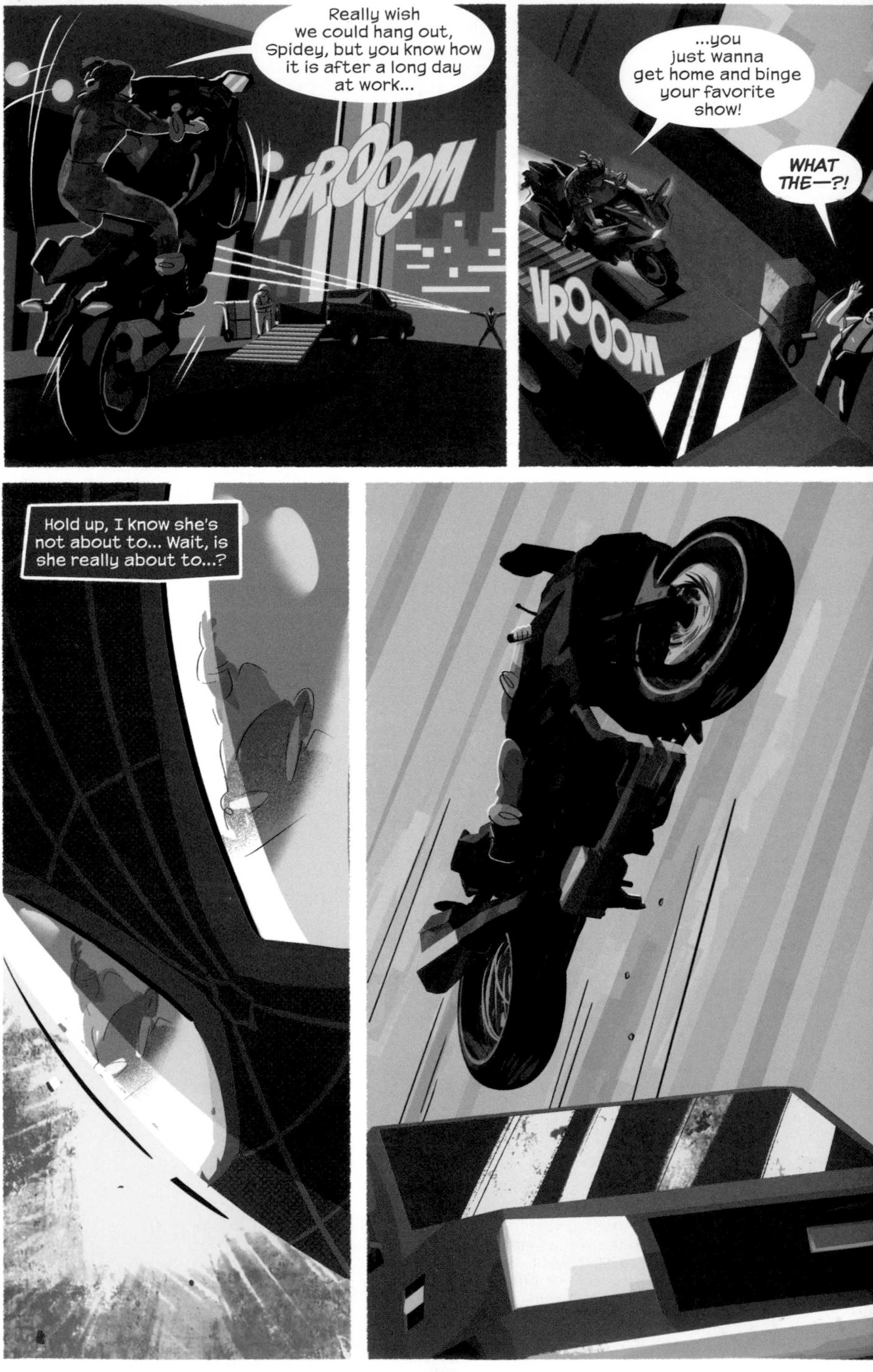
Really wish we could hang out, Spidey, but you know how it is after a long day at work...
VROOOM
...you just wanna get home and binge your favorite show!
WHAT THE—?!
VROOOM
Hold up, I know she's not about to... Wait, is she really about to...?

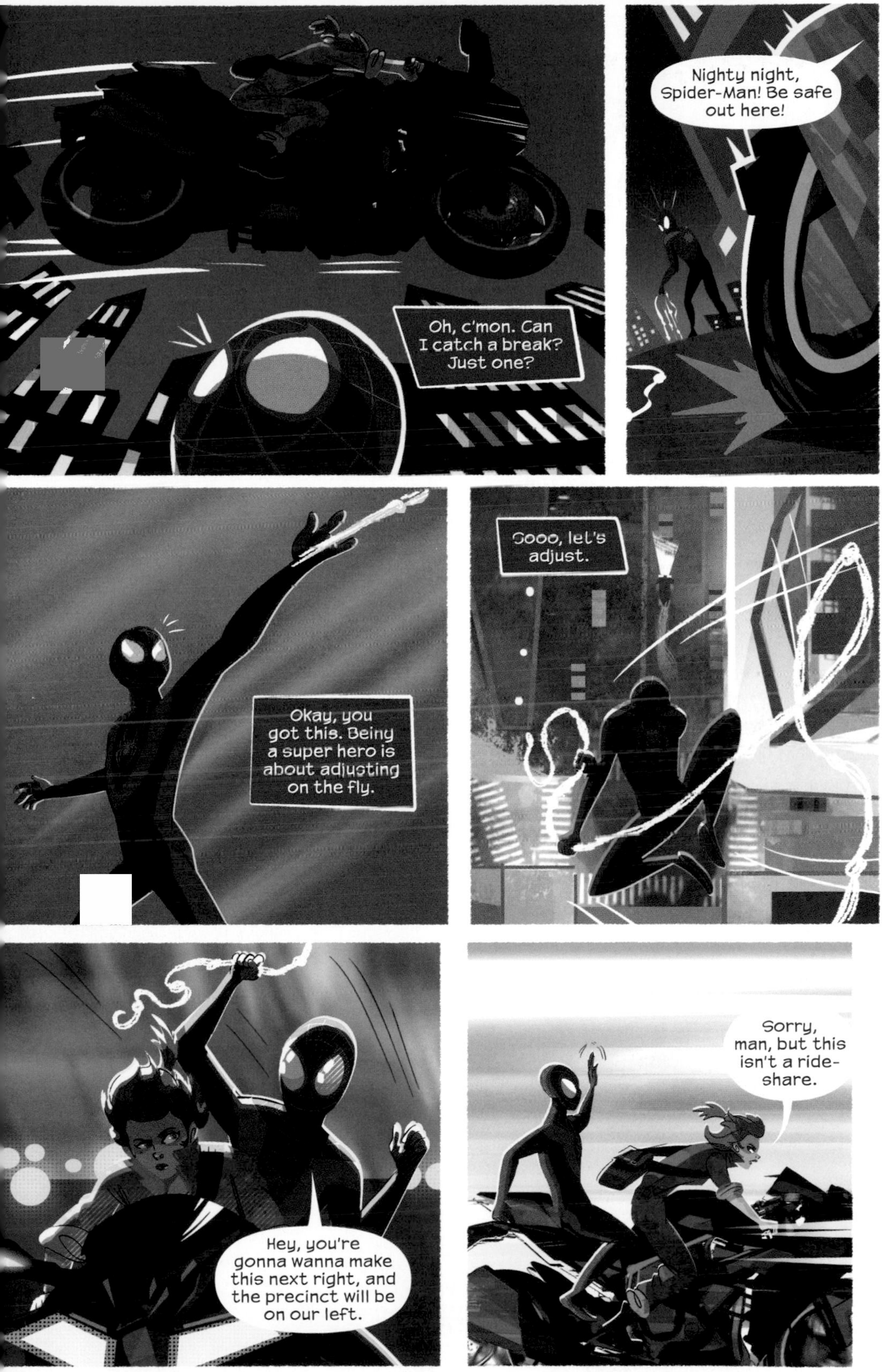
Oh, c'mon. Can I catch a break? Just one?
Nighty night, Spider-Man! Be safe out here!
Okay, you got this. Being a super hero is about adjusting on the fly.
Sooo, let's adjust.
Hey, you're gonna wanna make this next right, and the precinct will be on our left.
Sorry, man, but this isn't a ride-share.

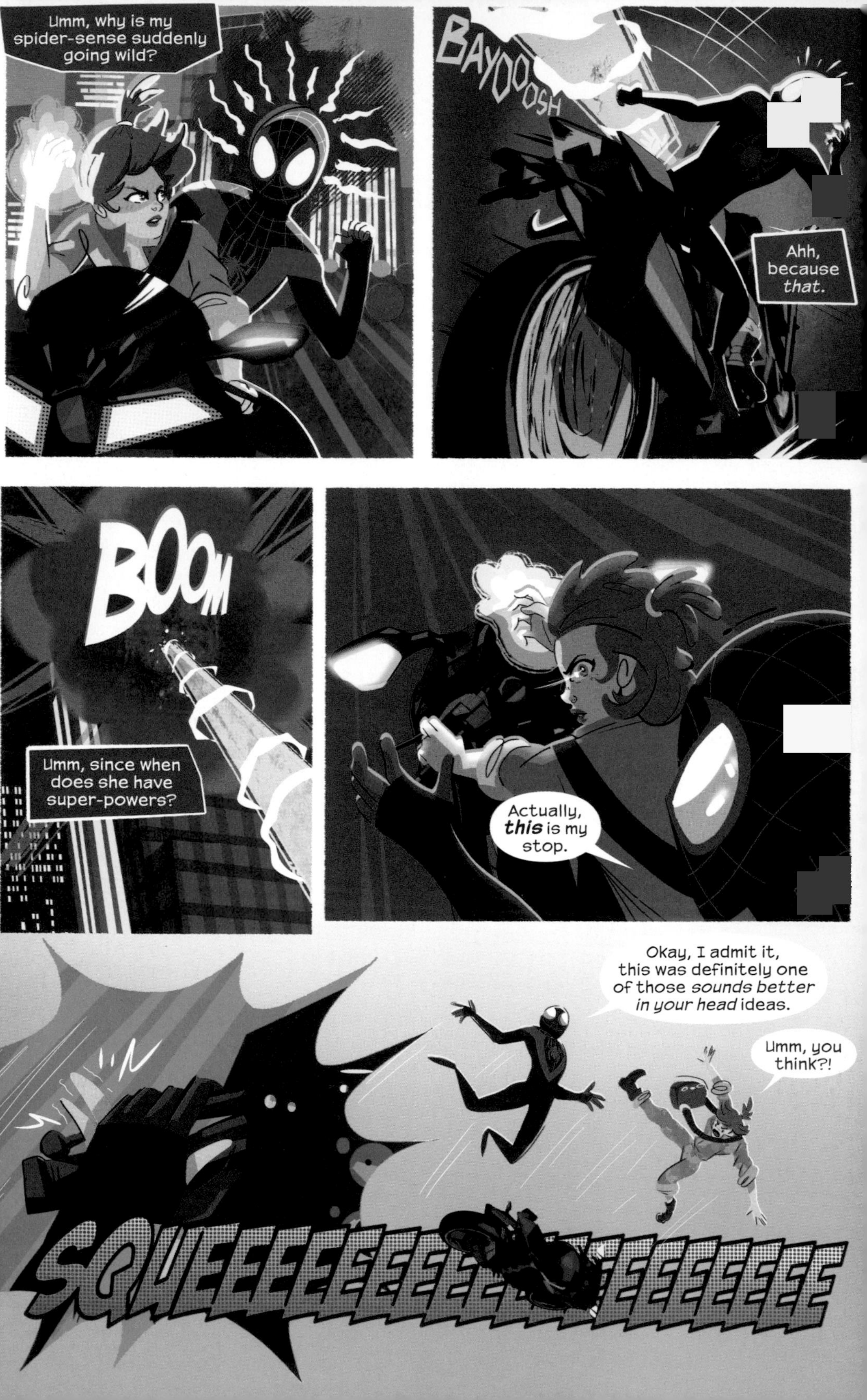
Umm, why is my spider-sense suddenly going wild?
BAYOOOSH
Ahh, because *that.*
BOOM
Umm, since when does she have super-powers?
Actually, ***this*** is my stop.
Okay, I admit it, this was definitely one of those *sounds better in your head* ideas.
Umm, you think?!
SQUEEEEEEEEEEEEEEEEEE

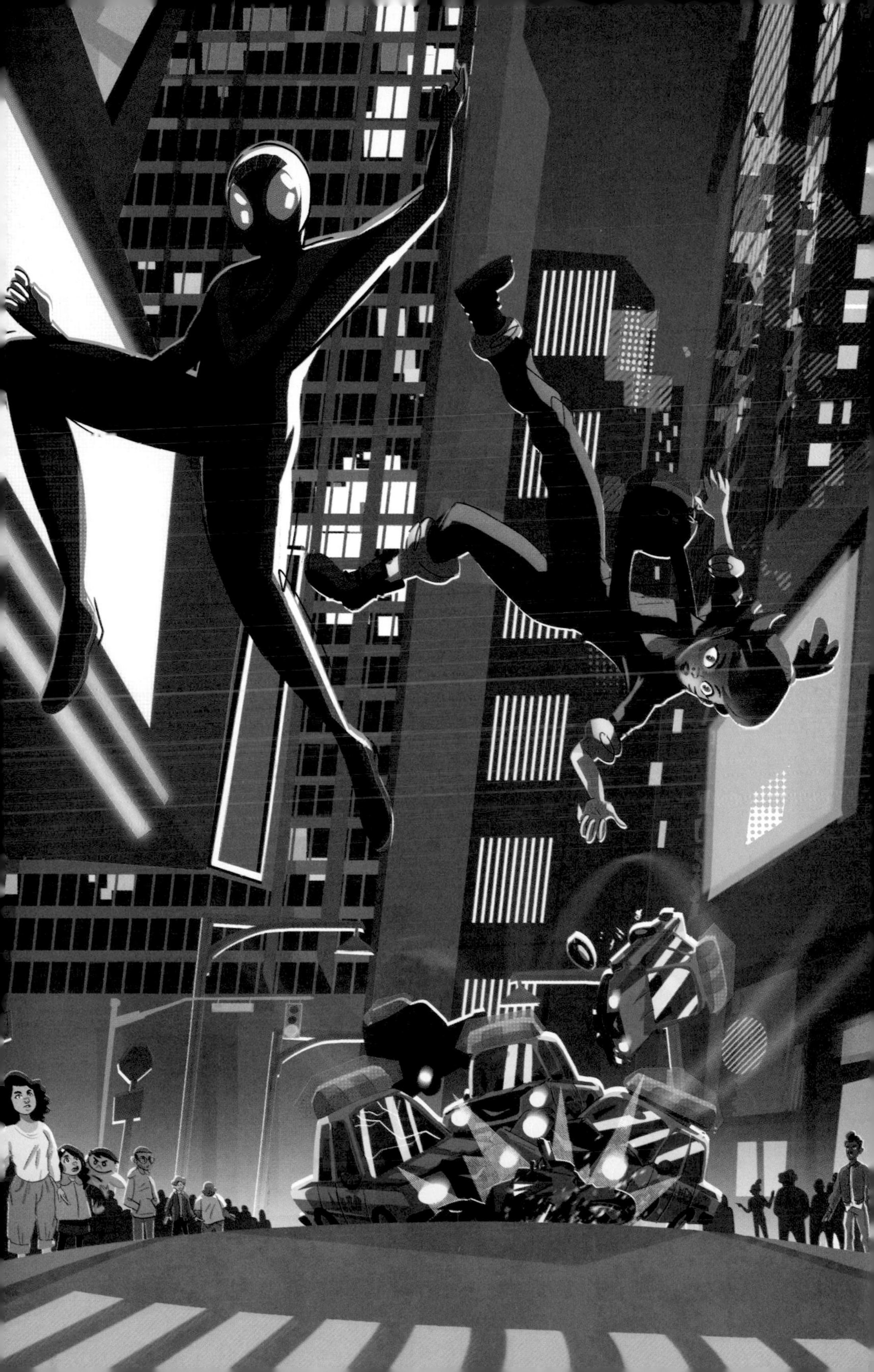

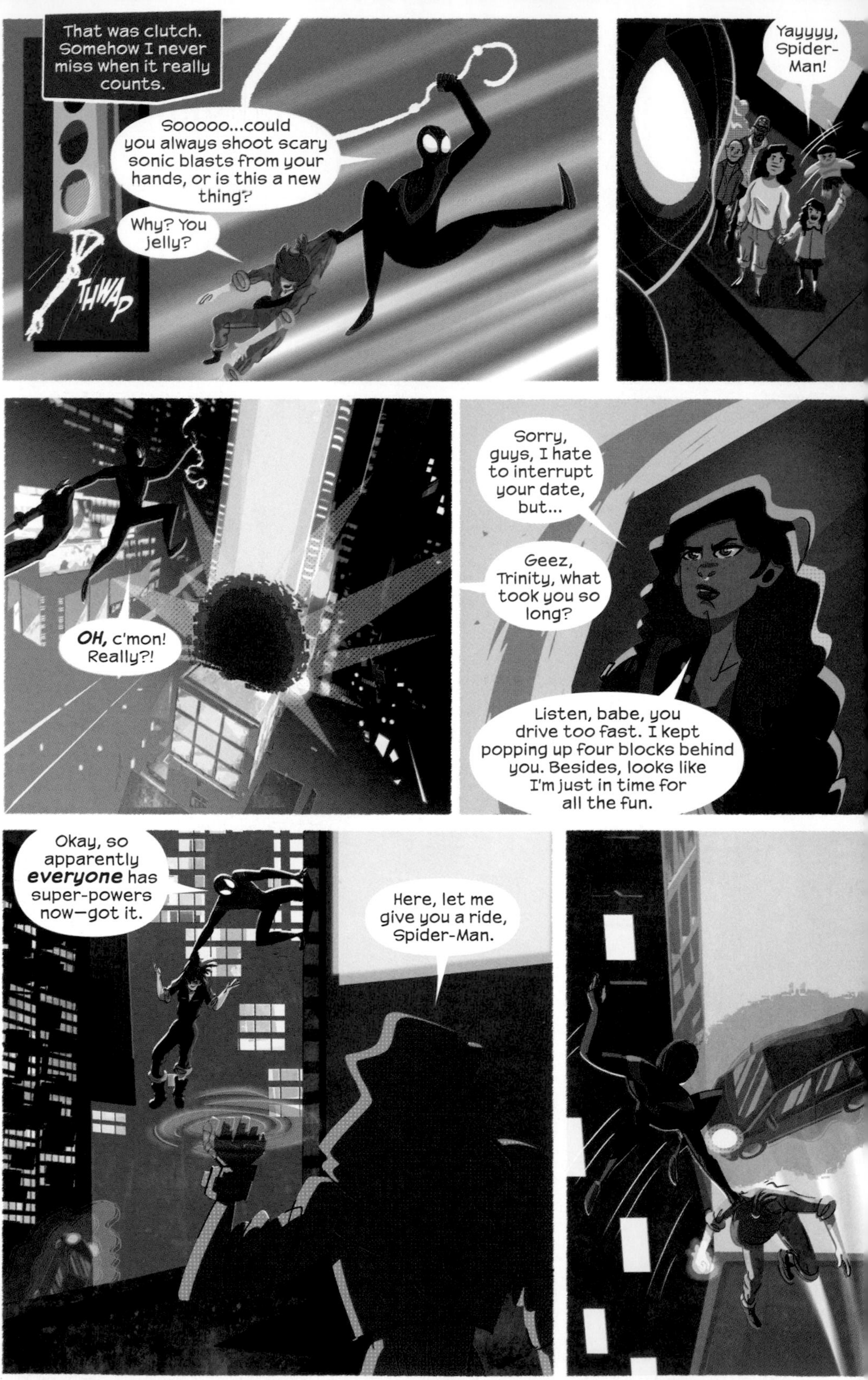
That was clutch. Somehow I never miss when it really counts.
Sooooo...could you always shoot scary sonic blasts from your hands, or is this a new thing?
Why? You jelly?
THWAP
Yayyyy, Spider-Man!
OH, c'mon! Really?!
Sorry, guys, I hate to interrupt your date, but...
Geez, Trinity, what took you so long?
Listen, babe, you drive too fast. I kept popping up four blocks behind you. Besides, looks like I'm just in time for all the fun.
Okay, so apparently everyone has super-powers now—got it.
Here, let me give you a ride, Spider-Man.

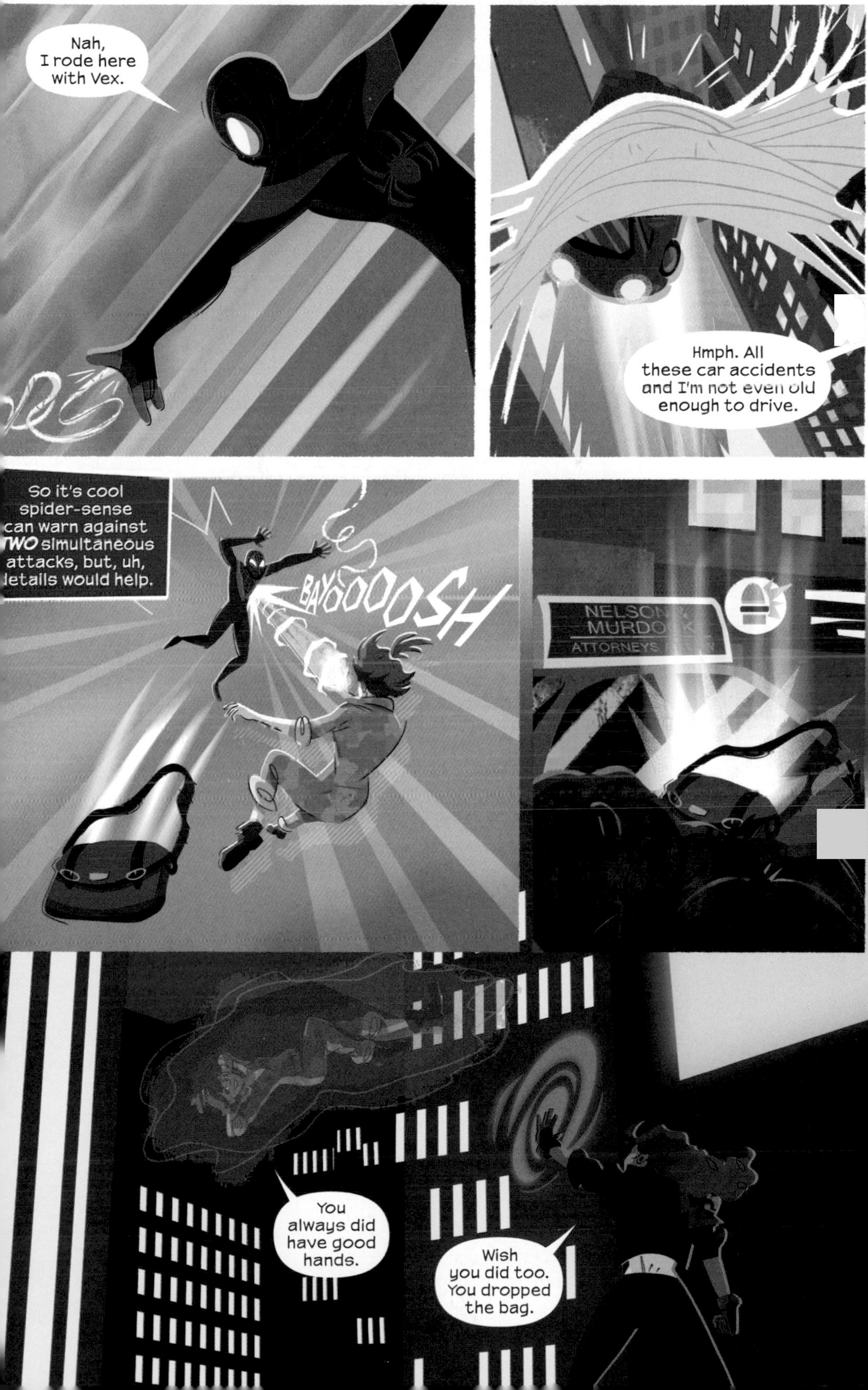

Nah, I rode here with Vex.
Hmph. All these car accidents and I'm not even old enough to drive.
So it's cool spider-sense can warn against **TWO** simultaneous attacks, but, uh, details would help.
BAYOOOOSH
NELSON & MURDOCK ATTORNEYS
You always did have good hands.
Wish you did too. You dropped the bag.

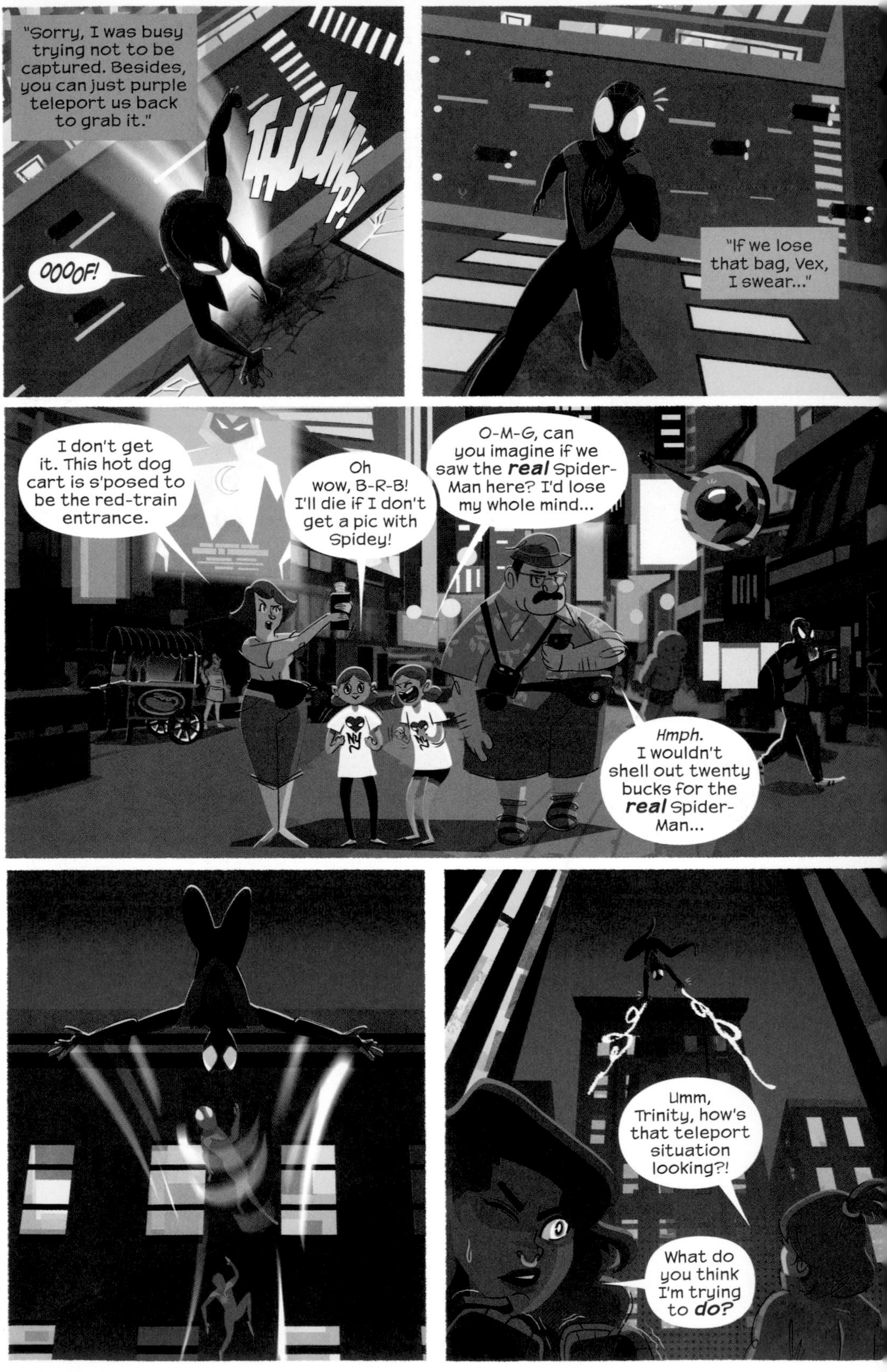
"Sorry, I was busy trying not to be captured. Besides, you can just purple teleport us back to grab it."
THUMP!
OOOOF!
"If we lose that bag, Vex, I swear..."
I don't get it. This hot dog cart is s'posed to be the red-train entrance.
Oh wow, B-R-B! I'll die if I don't get a pic with Spidey!
O-M-G, can you imagine if we saw the **real** Spider-Man here? I'd lose my whole mind...
Hmph. I wouldn't shell out twenty bucks for the **real** Spider-Man...
Umm, Trinity, how's that teleport situation looking?!
What do you think I'm trying to **do?**

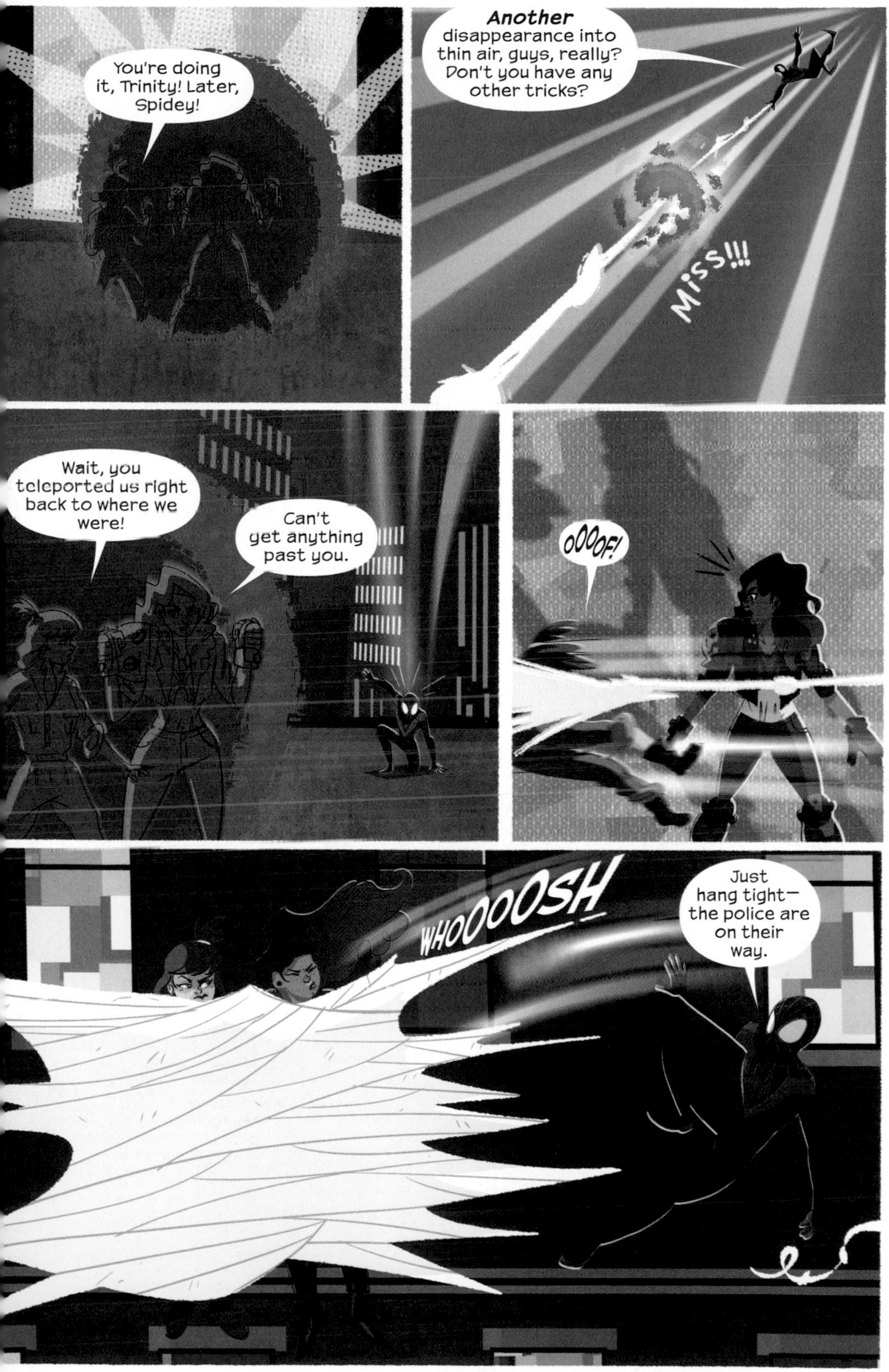
You're doing it, Trinity! Later, Spidey!
Another disappearance into thin air, guys, really? Don't you have any other tricks?
MISS!!!
Wait, you teleported us right back to where we were!
Can't get anything past you.
OOOOF!
WHOOOOOSH
Just hang tight— the police are on their way.

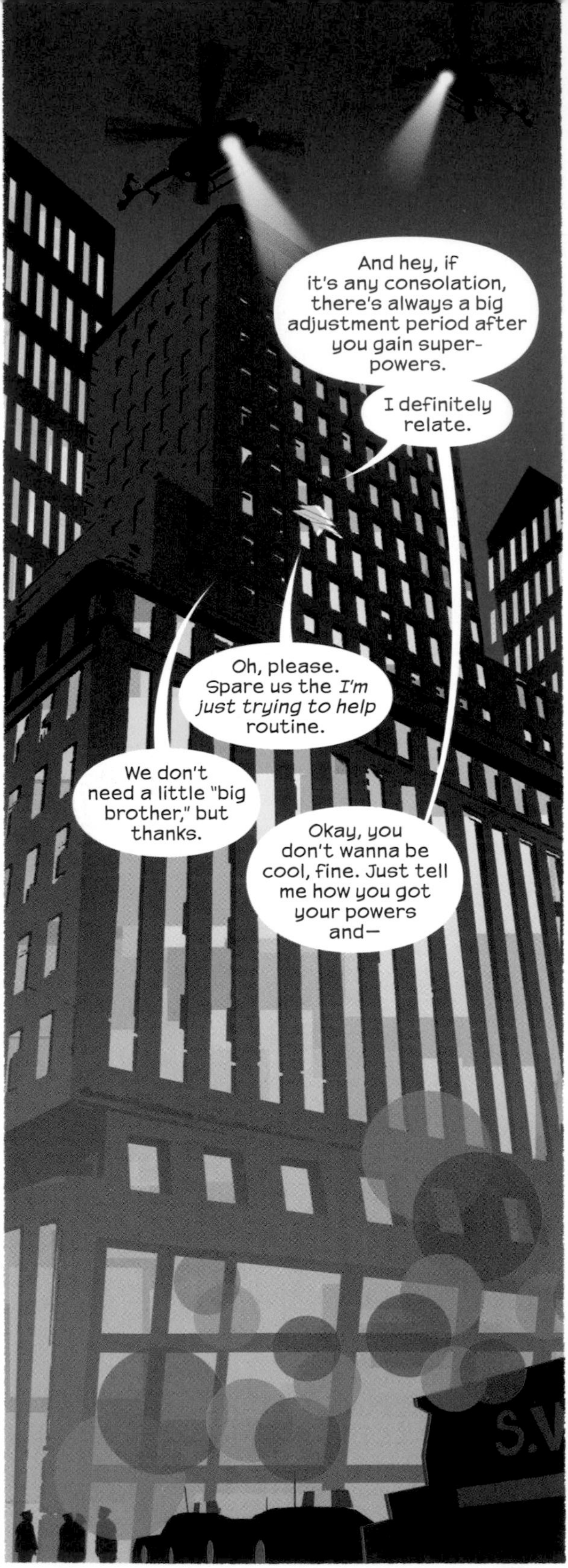
And hey, if it's any consolation, there's always a big adjustment period after you gain super-powers.
I definitely relate.
Oh, please. Spare us the *I'm just trying to help* routine.
We don't need a little "big brother," but thanks.
Okay, you don't wanna be cool, fine. Just tell me how you got your powers and—

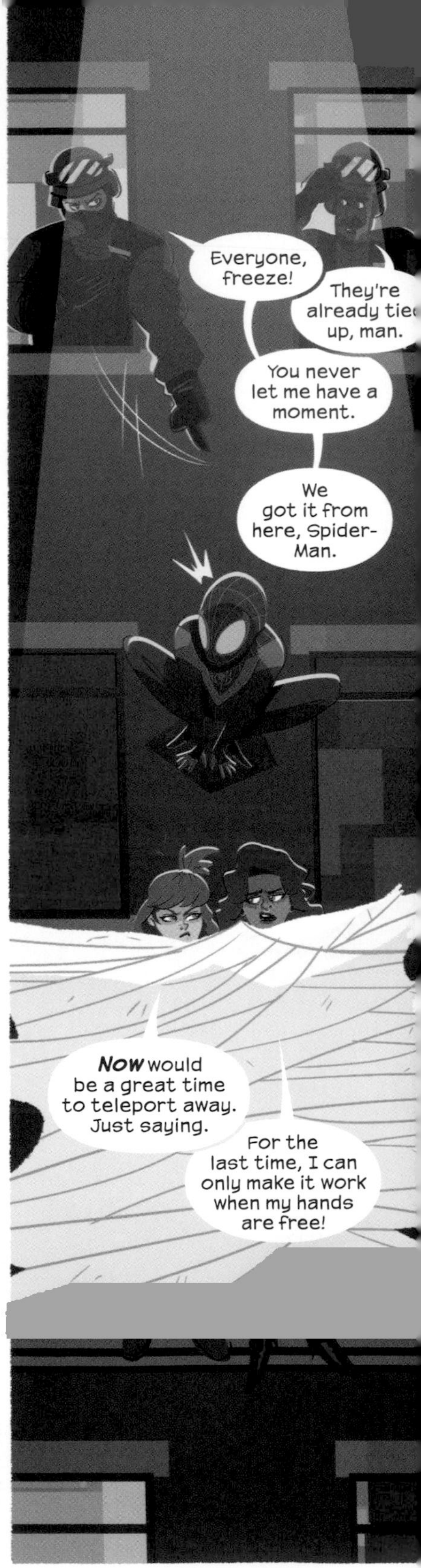
Everyone, freeze!
They're already tie up, man.
You never let me have a moment.
We got it from here, Spider-Man.
NOW would be a great time to teleport away. Just saying.
For the last time, I can only make it work when my hands are free!

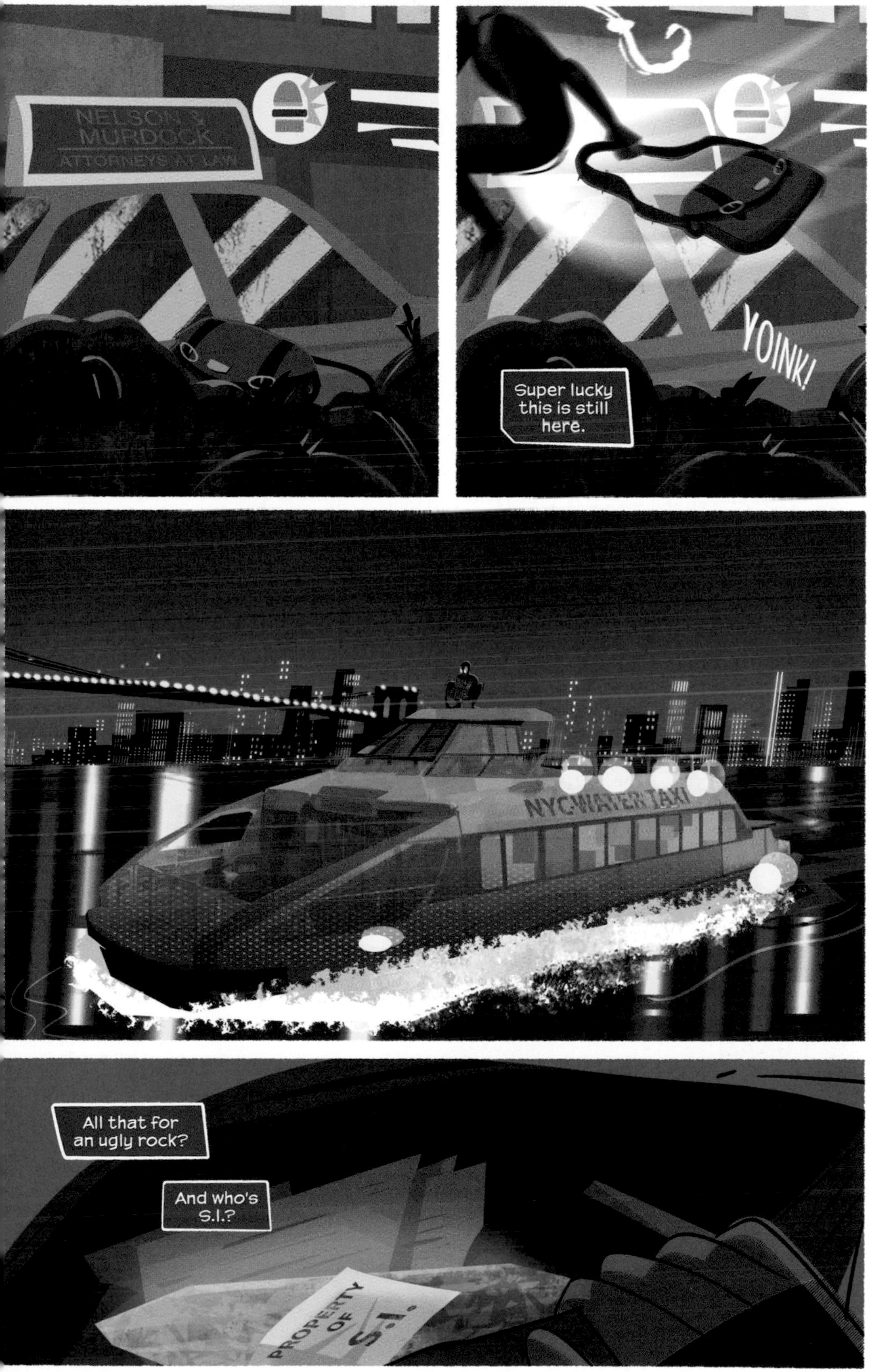
NELSON & MURDOCK
ATTORNEYS AT LAW
YOINK!
Super lucky this is still here.
NYC WATER TAXI
All that for an ugly rock?
And who's S.I.?
PROPERTY OF S.I.

CHAPTER
THREE

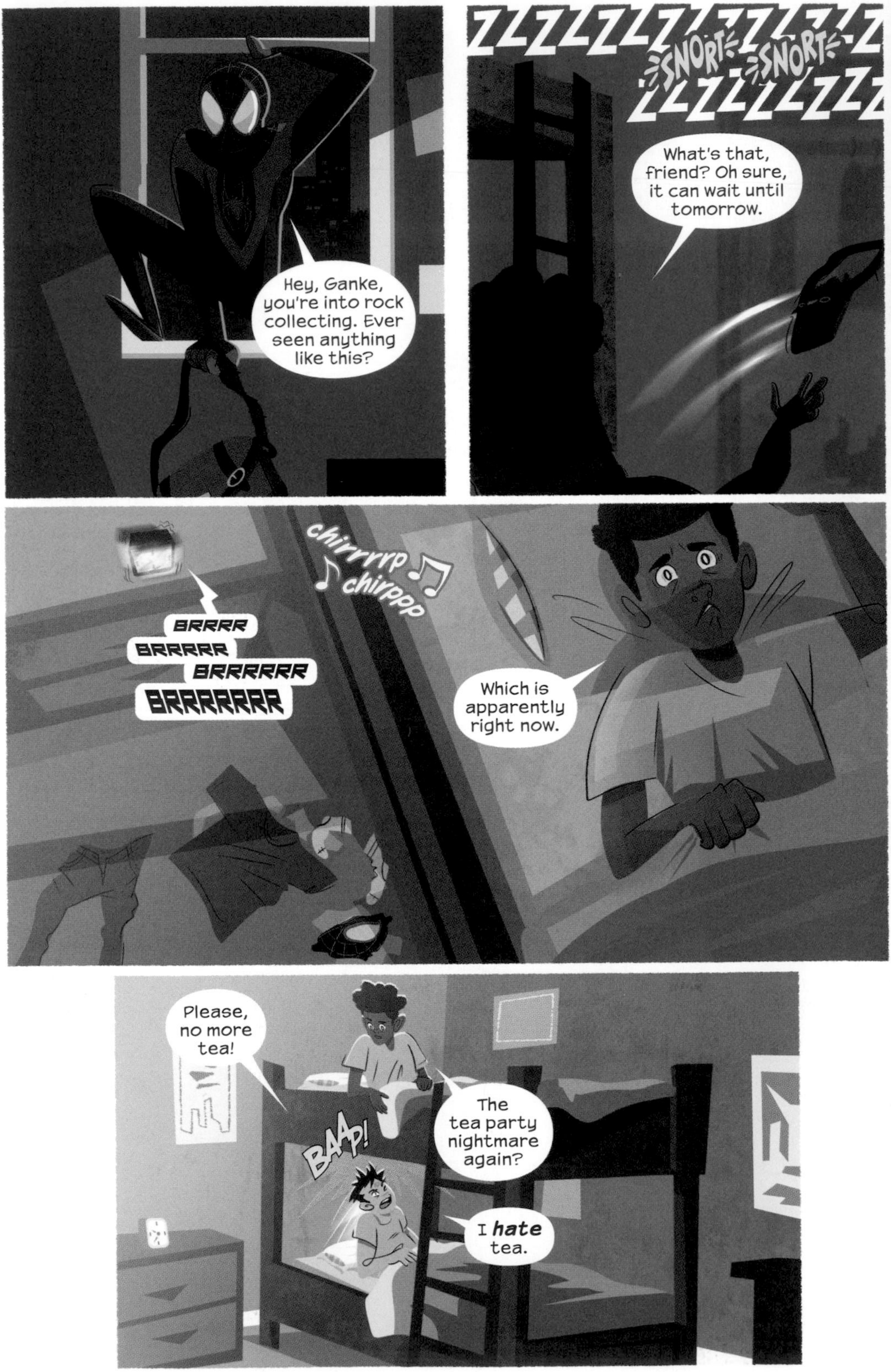
Hey, Ganke, you're into rock collecting. Ever seen anything like this?
ZZZZZZZ SNORT ZZZZ SNORT ZZ
ZZZZZZZZZZ
What's that, friend? Oh sure, it can wait until tomorrow.
BRRRR
BRRRRR
BRRRRRR
BRRRRRRR
chirrrrp
chirppp
Which is apparently right now.
Please, no more tea!
The tea party nightmare again?
BAAP!
I *hate* tea.

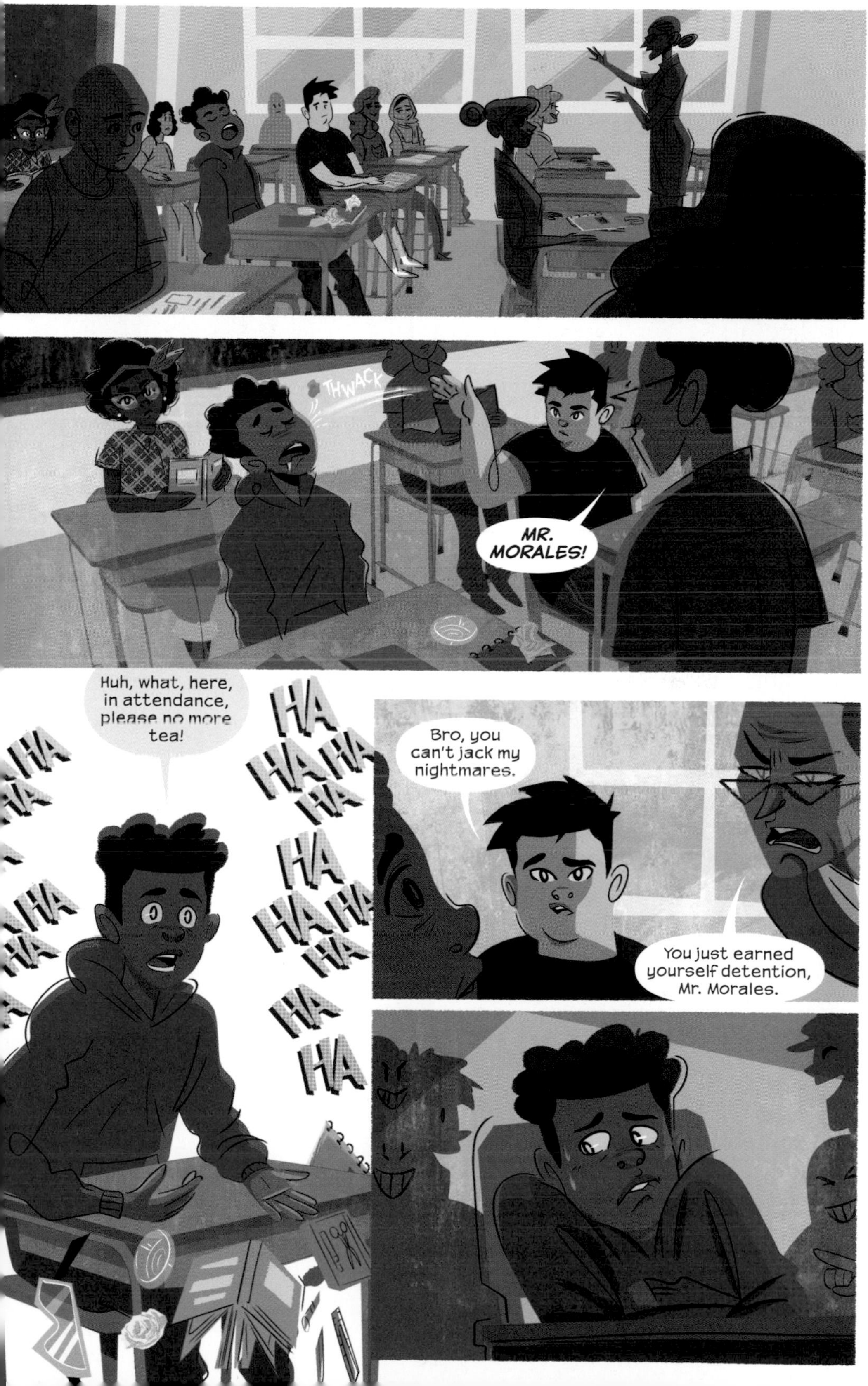
THWACK
MR. MORALES!
Huh, what, here, in attendance, please no more tea!
HA HA HA HA HA HA HA HA HA HA HA HA HA HA HA HA HA HA
Bro, you can't jack my nightmares.
You just earned yourself detention, Mr. Morales.

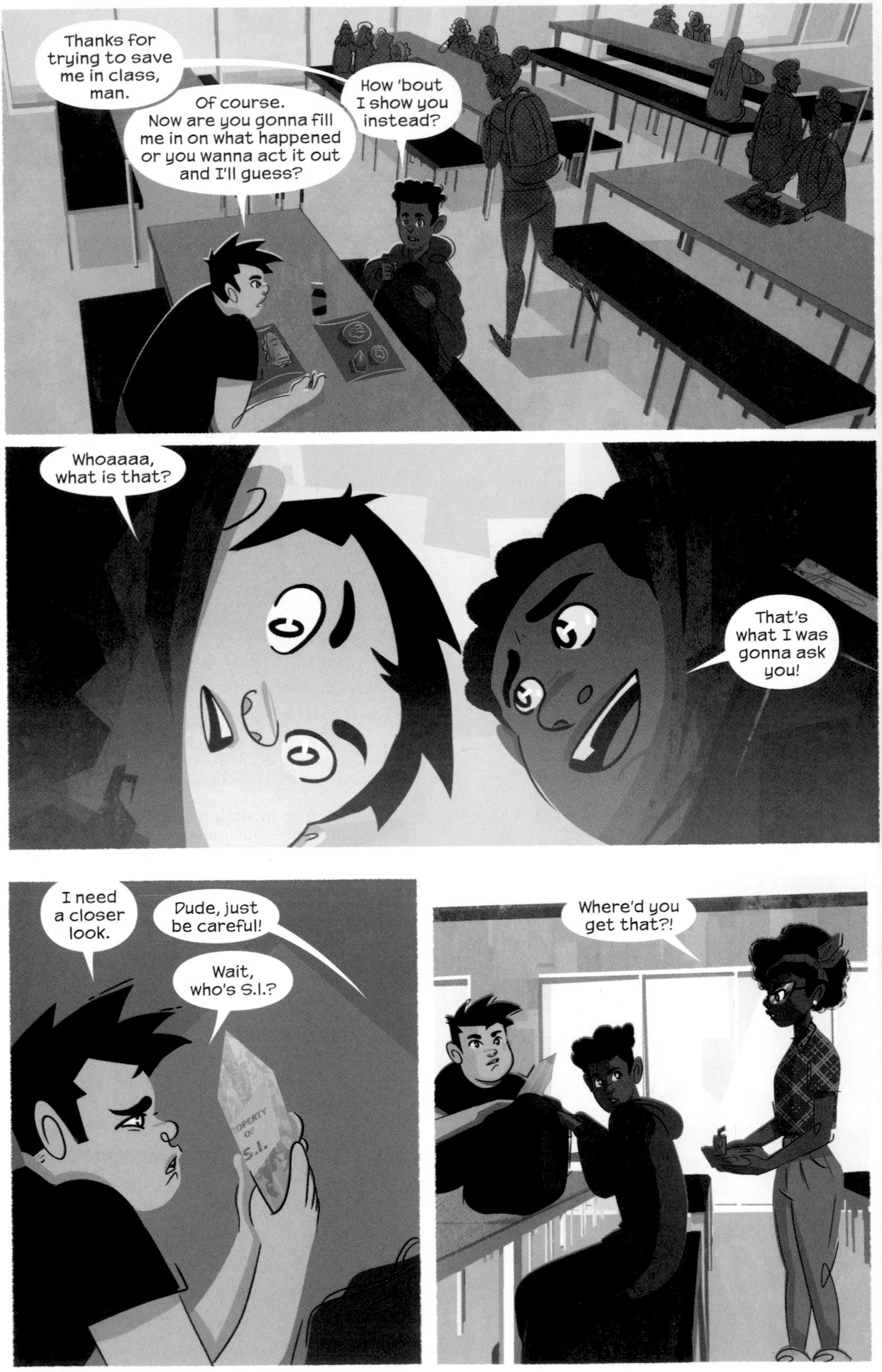
Thanks for trying to save me in class, man.
Of course. Now are you gonna fill me in on what happened or you wanna act it out and I'll guess?
How 'bout I show you instead?
Whoaaaa, what is that?
That's what I was gonna ask you!
I need a closer look.
Dude, just be careful!
Wait, who's S.I.?
PROPERTY OF S.I.
Where'd you get that?!

43

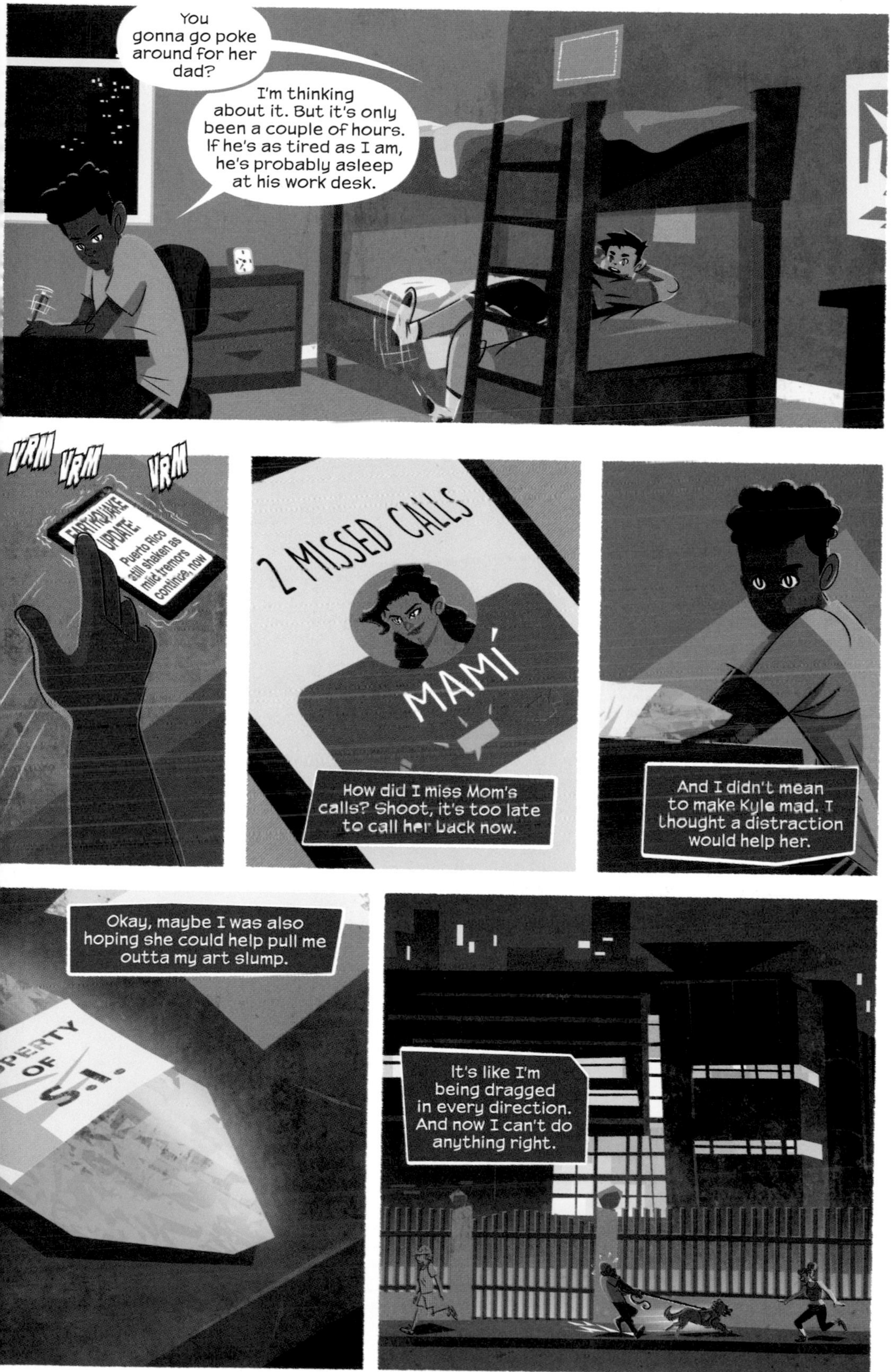
You gonna go poke around for her dad?
I'm thinking about it. But it's only been a couple of hours. If he's as tired as I am, he's probably asleep at his work desk.
VRM VRM VRM
EARTHQUAKE UPDATE:
Puerto Rico still shaken as mild tremors continue, now
2 MISSED CALLS
MAMÍ
How did I miss Mom's calls? Shoot, it's too late to call her back now.
And I didn't mean to make Kyle mad. I thought a distraction would help her.
Okay, maybe I was also hoping she could help pull me outta my art slump.
PERTY OF S.I.
It's like I'm being dragged in every direction. And now I can't do anything right.

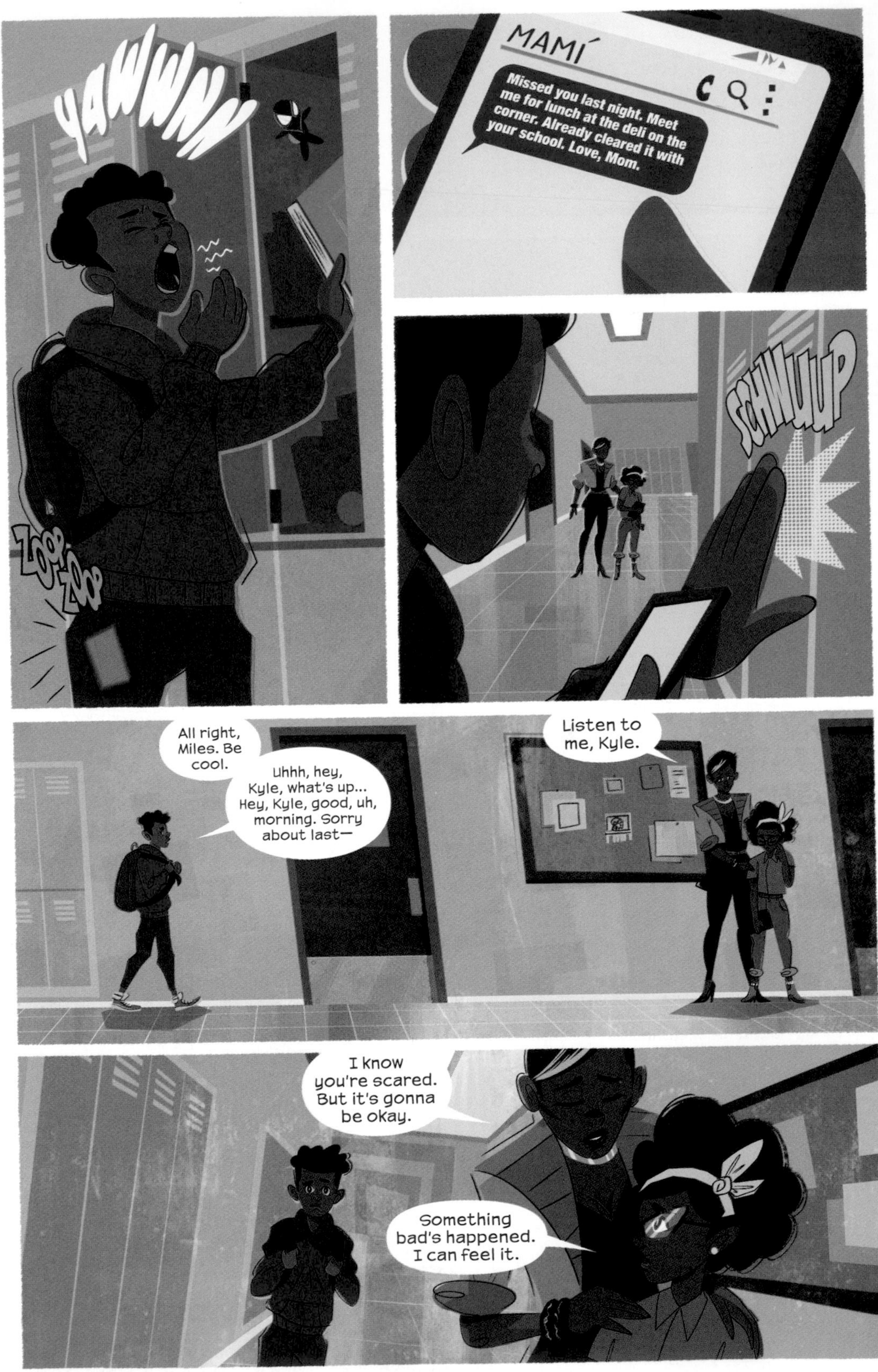
YAWWWN
ZOOP ZOOP
MAMÍ
Missed you last night. Meet me for lunch at the deli on the corner. Already cleared it with your school. Love, Mom.
SCHWUUP
All right, Miles. Be cool.
Uhhh, hey, Kyle, what's up... Hey, Kyle, good, uh, morning. Sorry about last—
Listen to me, Kyle.
I know you're scared. But it's gonna be okay.
Something bad's happened. I can feel it.

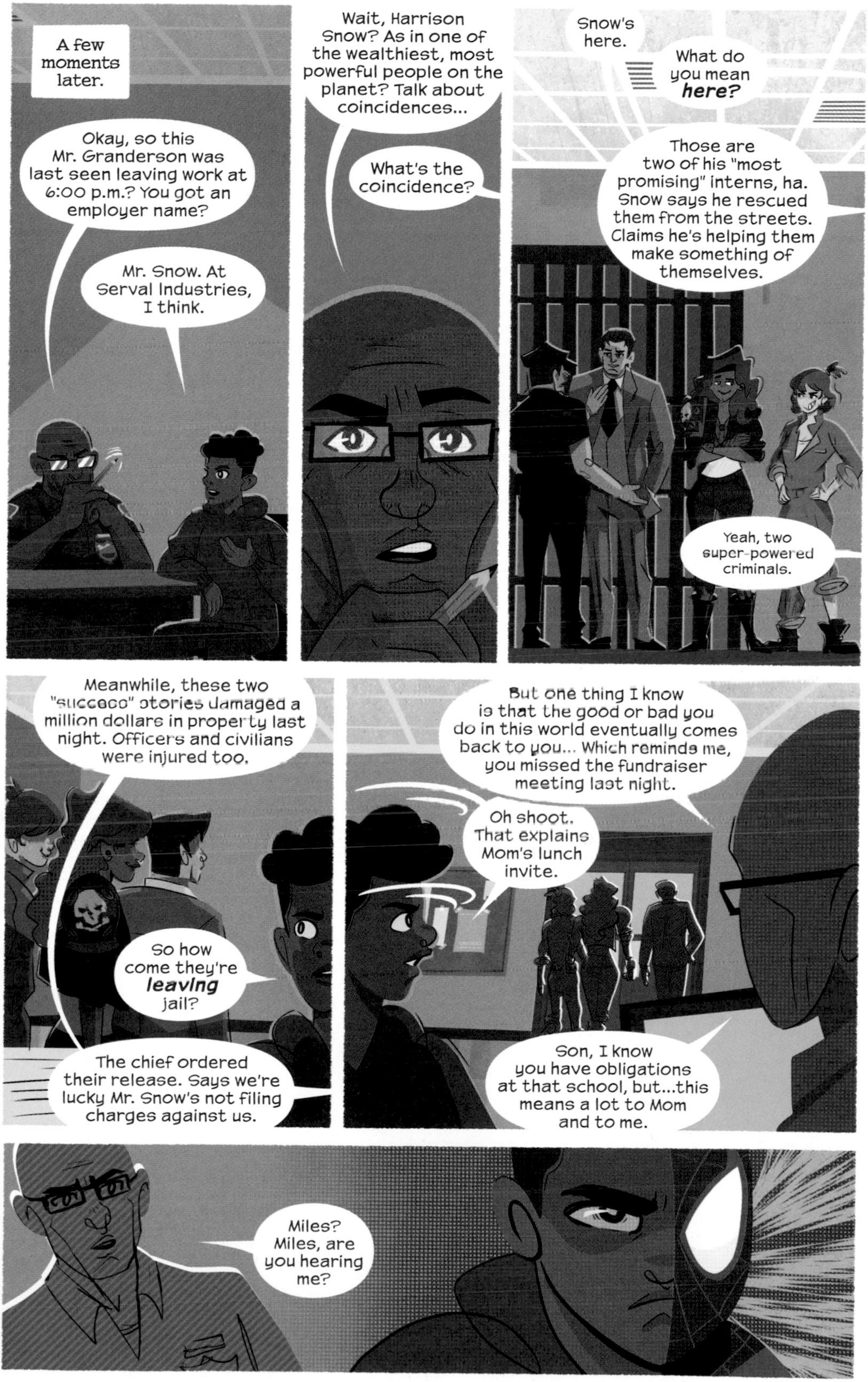

A few moments later.
Okay, so this Mr. Granderson was last seen leaving work at 6:00 p.m.? You got an employer name?
Mr. Snow. At Serval Industries, I think.
Wait, Harrison Snow? As in one of the wealthiest, most powerful people on the planet? Talk about coincidences...
What's the coincidence?
Snow's here.
What do you mean *here?*
Those are two of his "most promising" interns, ha. Snow says he rescued them from the streets. Claims he's helping them make something of themselves.
Yeah, two super-powered criminals.
Meanwhile, these two "success" stories damaged a million dollars in property last night. Officers and civilians were injured too.
So how come they're *leaving* jail?
The chief ordered their release. Says we're lucky Mr. Snow's not filing charges against us.
But one thing I know is that the good or bad you do in this world eventually comes back to you... Which reminds me, you missed the fundraiser meeting last night.
Oh shoot. That explains Mom's lunch invite.
Son, I know you have obligations at that school, but...this means a lot to Mom and to me.
Miles? Miles, are you hearing me?

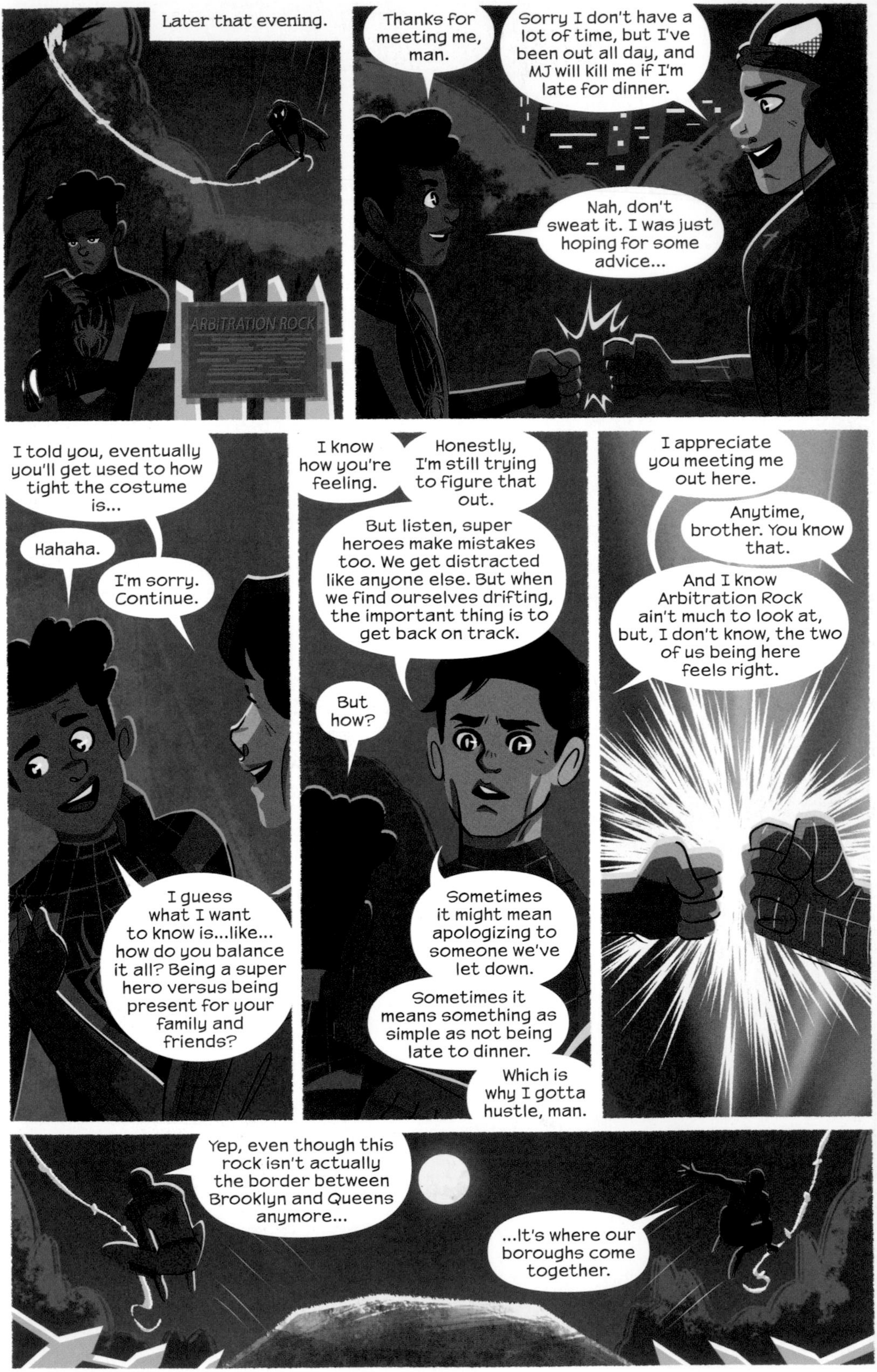
Later that evening.
ARBITRATION ROCK
Thanks for meeting me, man.
Sorry I don't have a lot of time, but I've been out all day, and MJ will kill me if I'm late for dinner.
Nah, don't sweat it. I was just hoping for some advice...
I told you, eventually you'll get used to how tight the costume is...
Hahaha.
I'm sorry. Continue.
I guess what I want to know is...like... how do you balance it all? Being a super hero versus being present for your family and friends?
I know how you're feeling.
Honestly, I'm still trying to figure that out.
But listen, super heroes make mistakes too. We get distracted like anyone else. But when we find ourselves drifting, the important thing is to get back on track.
But how?
Sometimes it might mean apologizing to someone we've let down.
Sometimes it means something as simple as not being late to dinner.
Which is why I gotta hustle, man.
I appreciate you meeting me out here.
Anytime, brother. You know that.
And I know Arbitration Rock ain't much to look at, but, I don't know, the two of us being here feels right.
Yep, even though this rock isn't actually the border between Brooklyn and Queens anymore...
...It's where our boroughs come together.

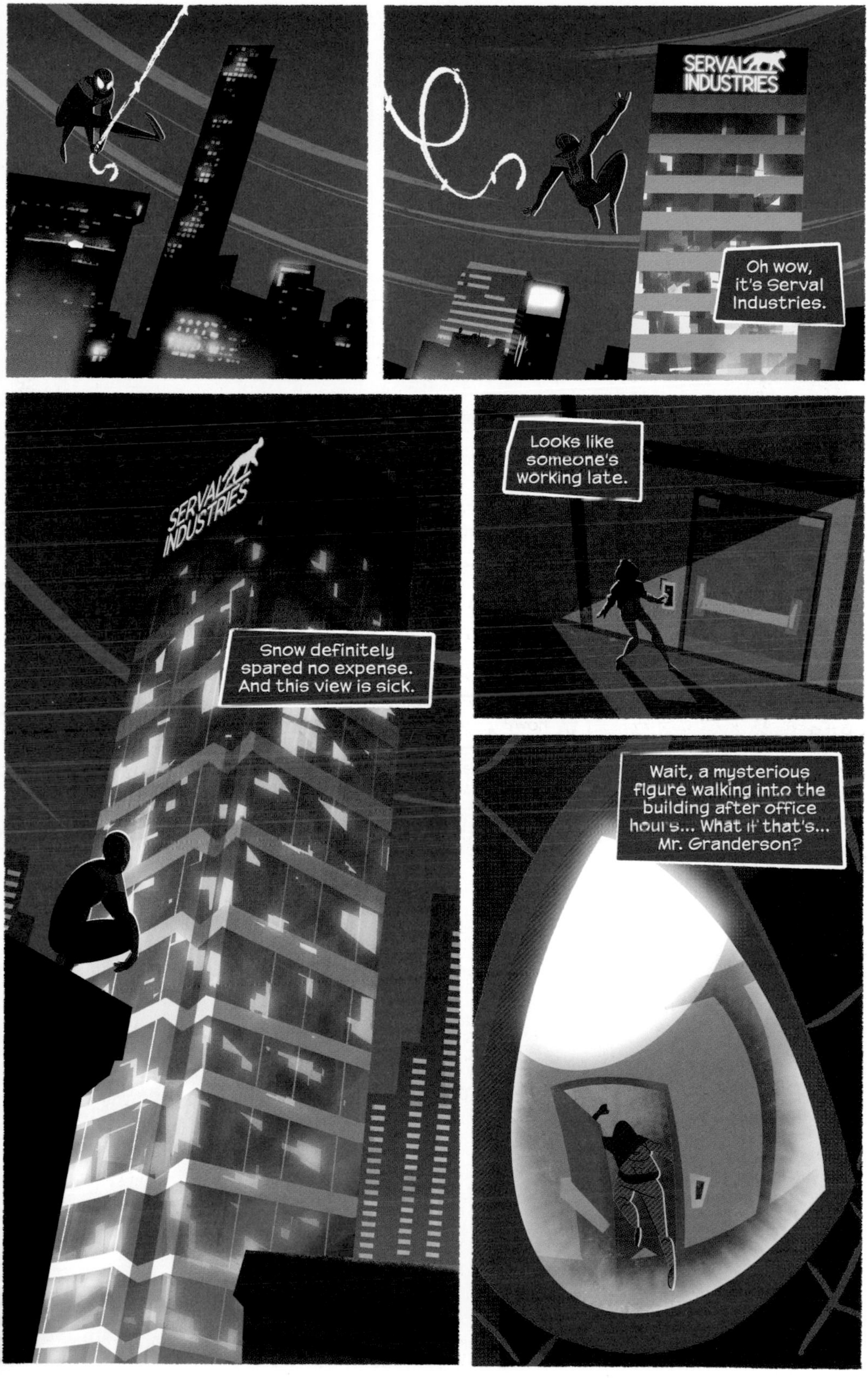
SERVAL INDUSTRIES
Oh wow, it's Serval Industries.
SERVAL INDUSTRIES
Snow definitely spared no expense. And this view is sick.
Looks like someone's working late.
Wait, a mysterious figure walking into the building after office hours... What if that's... Mr. Granderson?

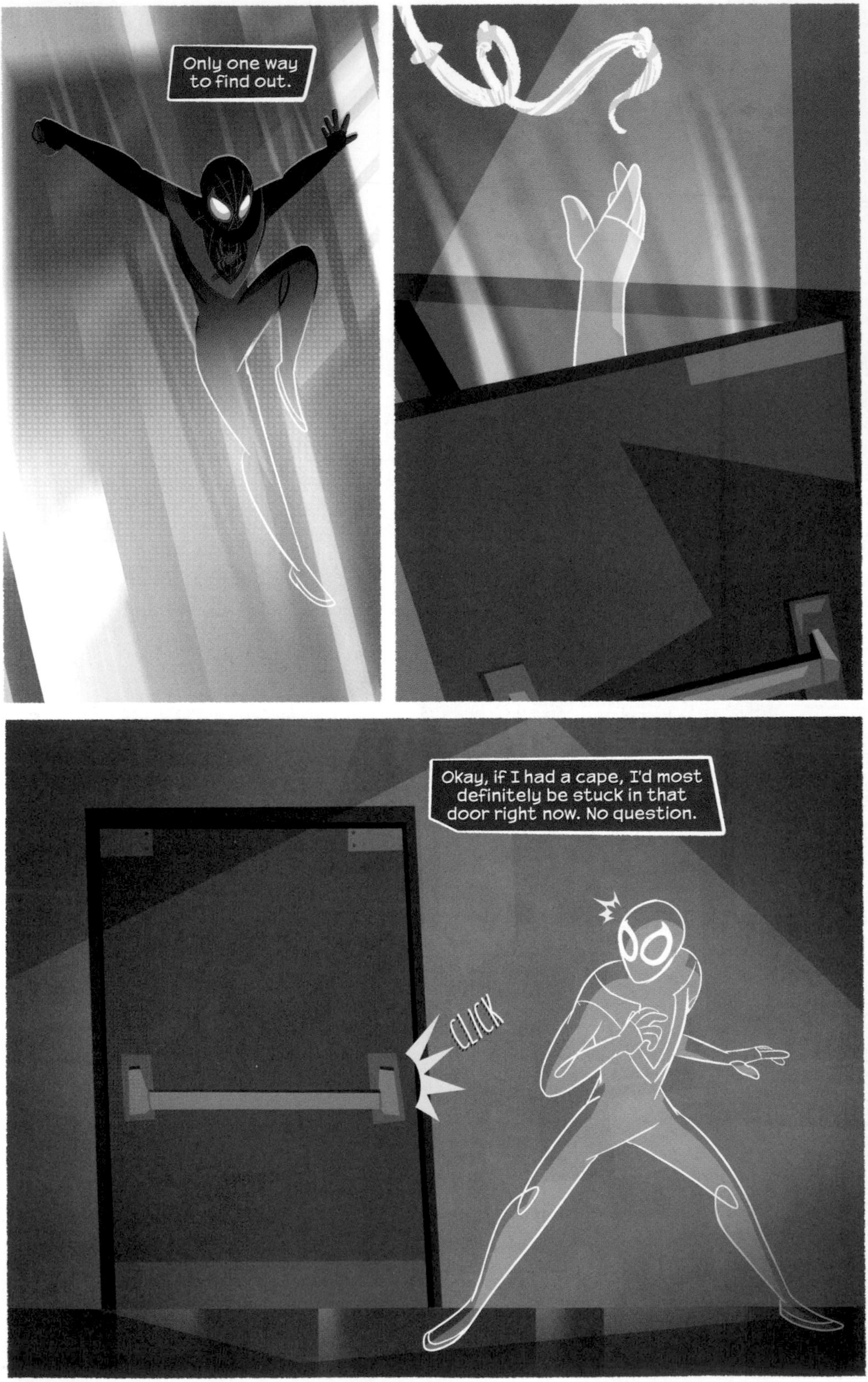
Only one way to find out.
Okay, if I had a cape, I'd most definitely be stuck in that door right now. No question.
CLICK

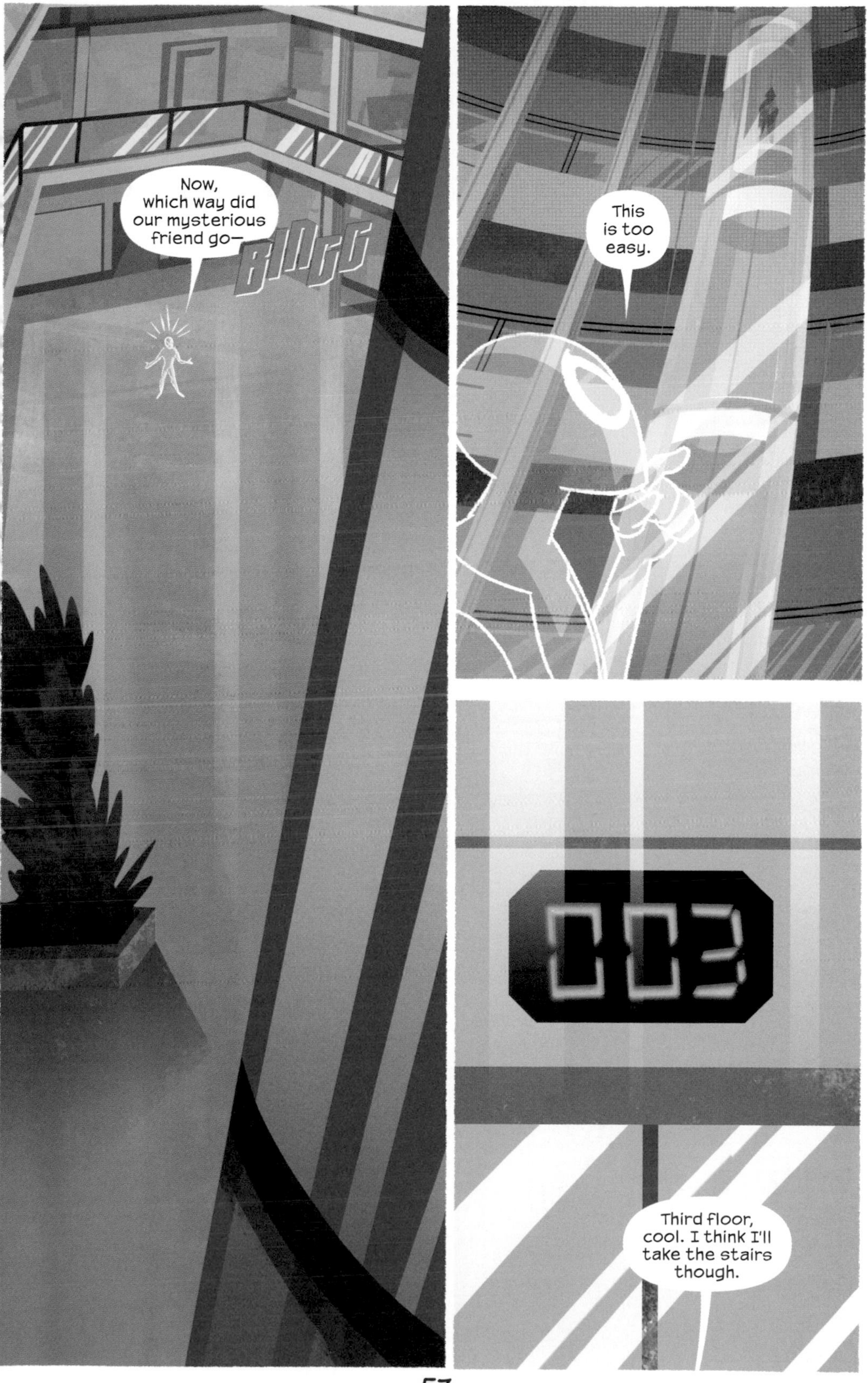
Now, which way did our mysterious friend go—
BINGG
This is too easy.
003
Third floor, cool. I think I'll take the stairs though.

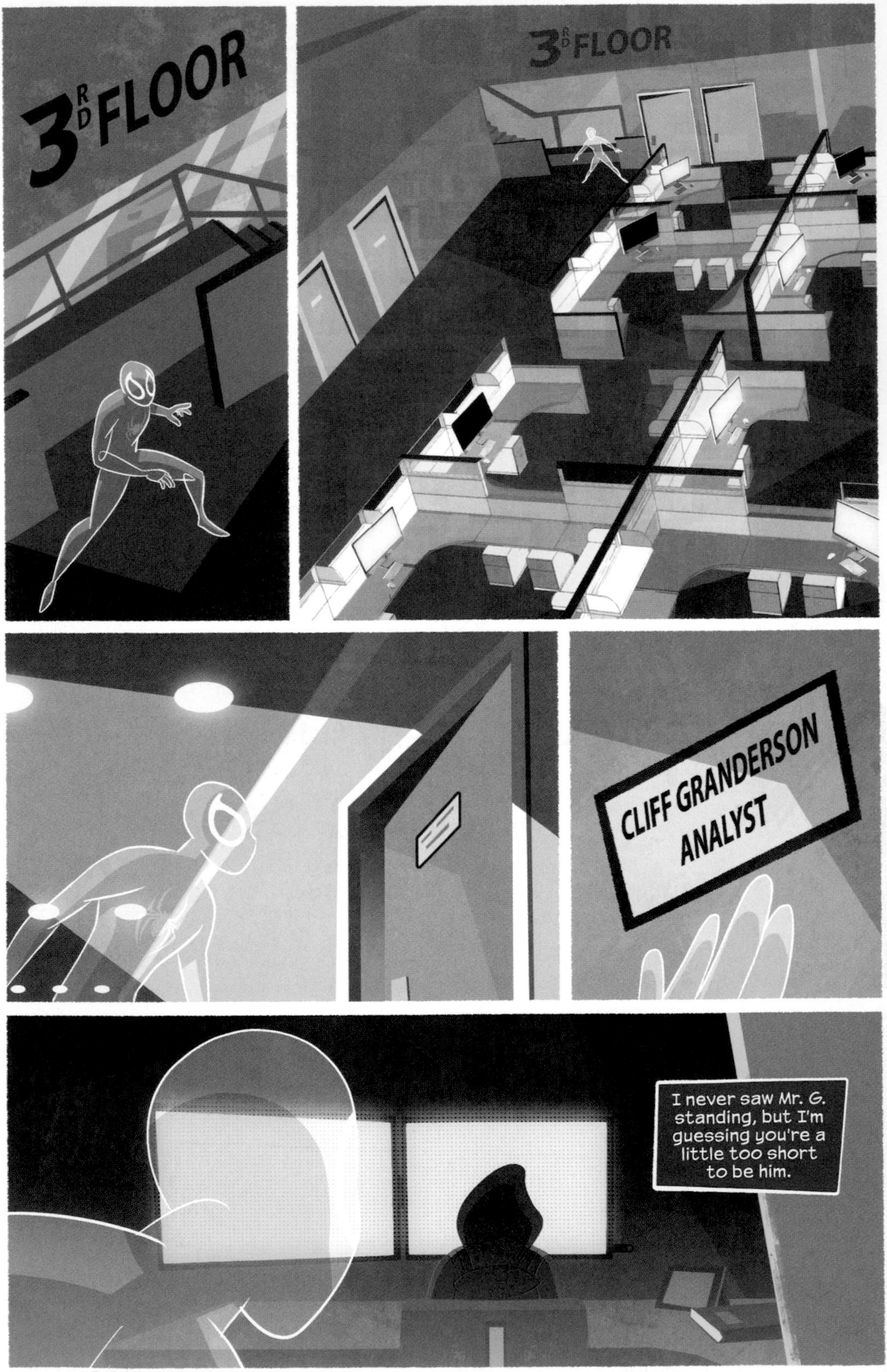
3RD FLOOR
3RD FLOOR
CLIFF GRANDERSON
ANALYST
I never saw Mr. G. standing, but I'm guessing you're a little too short to be him.

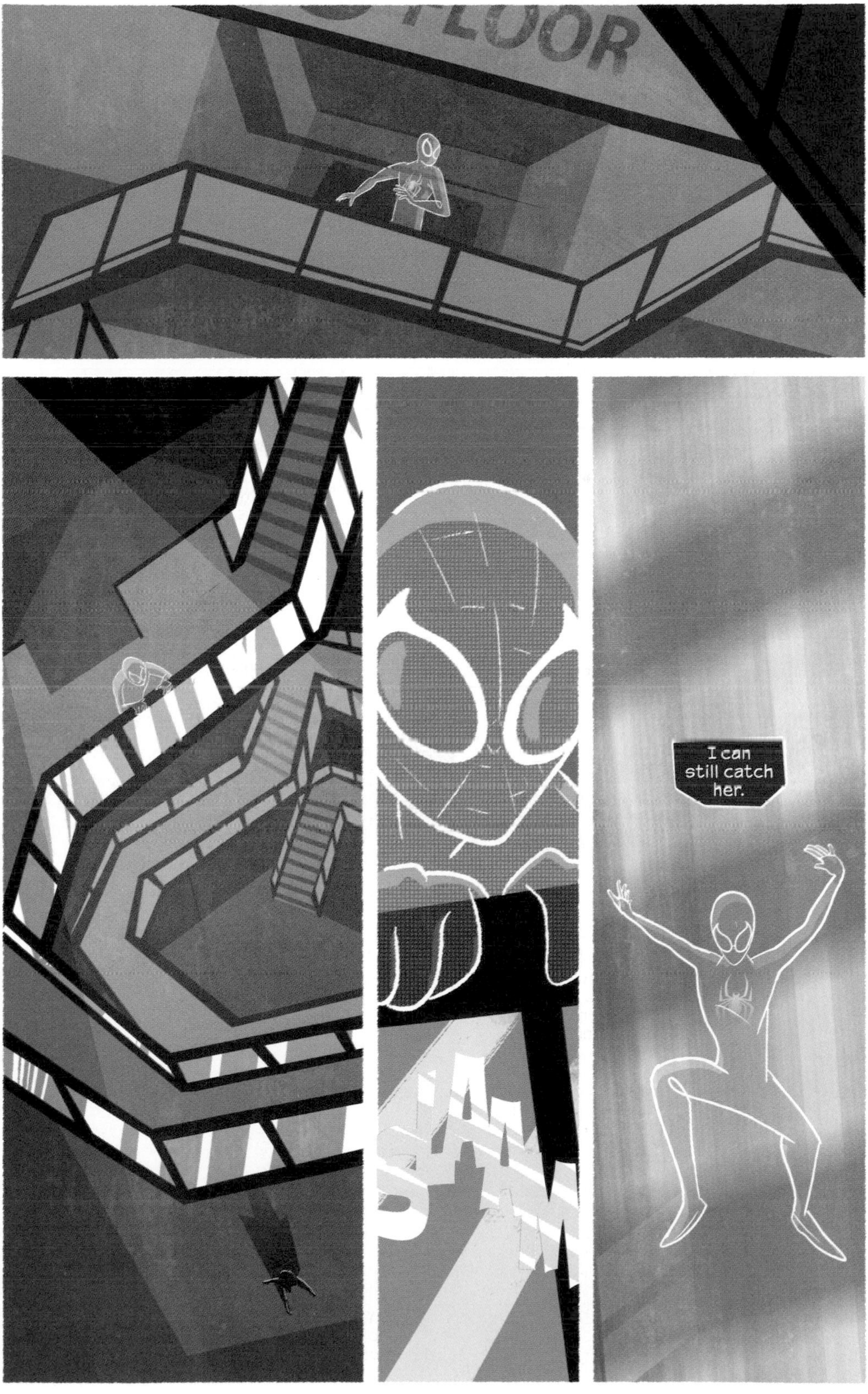
FLOOR
I can still catch her.

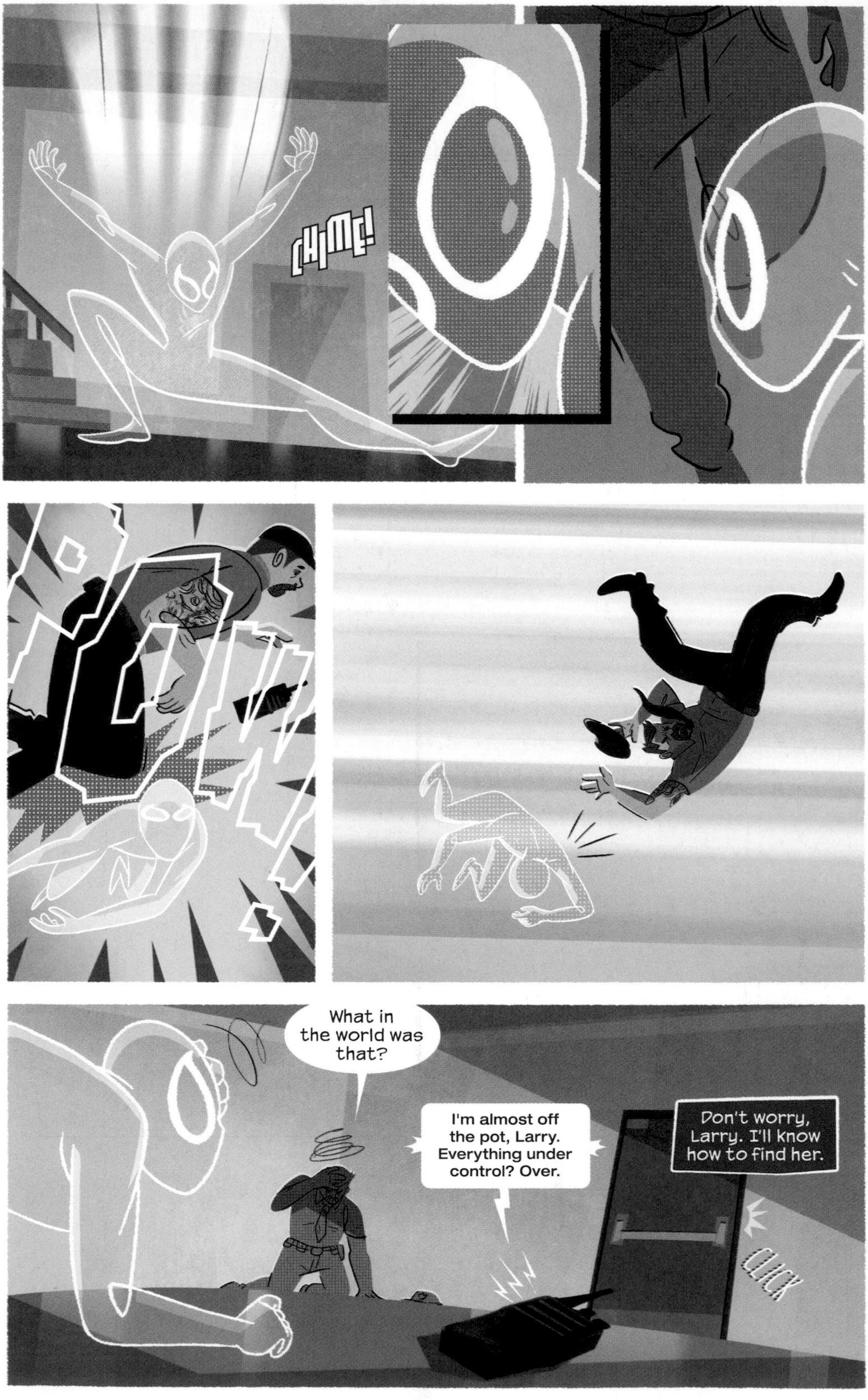
CHIME!
What in the world was that?
I'm almost off the pot, Larry. Everything under control? Over.
Don't worry, Larry. I'll know how to find her.
CLICK

CHAPTER

FOUR

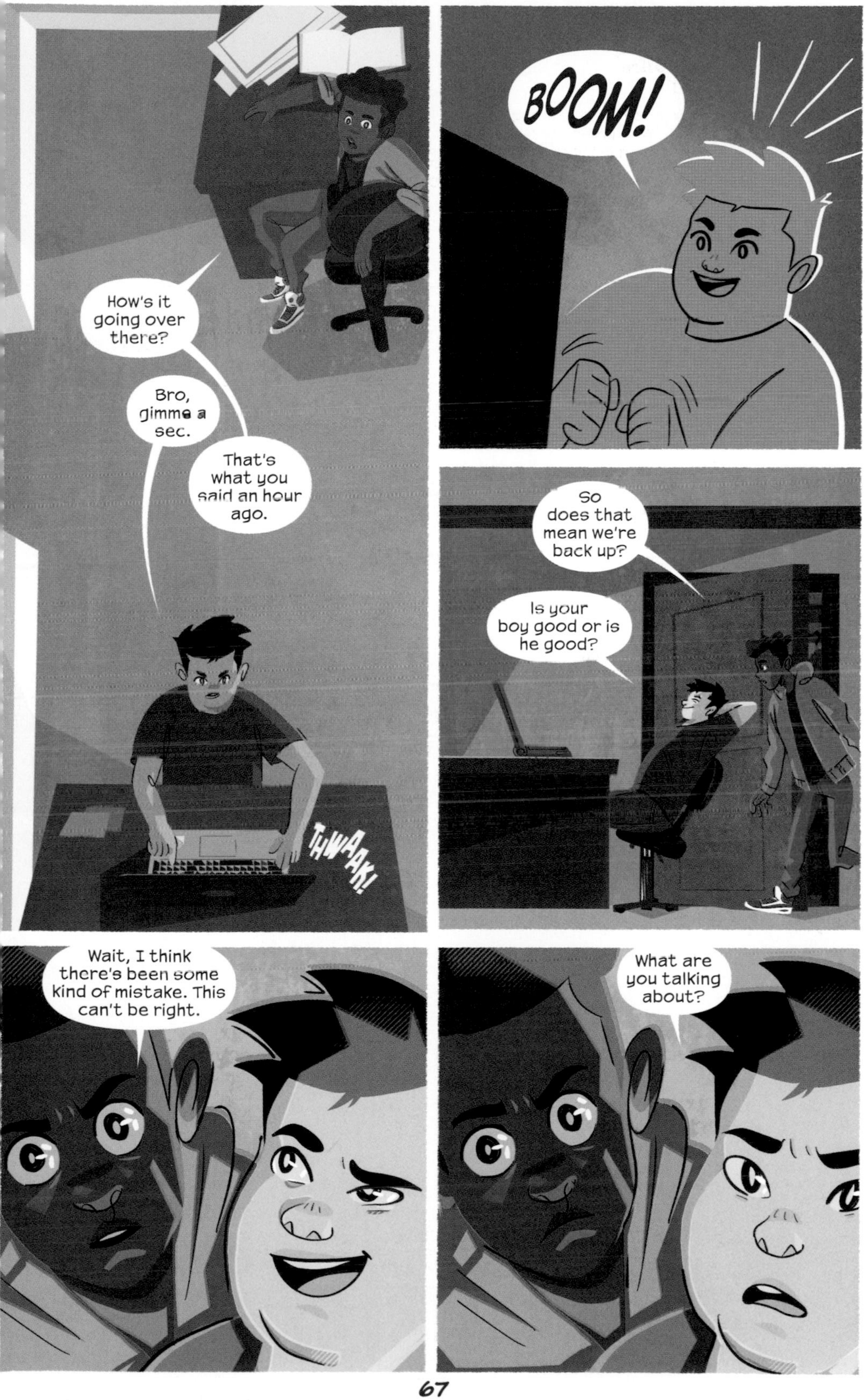
How's it going over there?
Bro, gimme a sec.
That's what you said an hour ago.
THWAAK!
BOOM!
So does that mean we're back up?
Is your boy good or is he good?
Wait, I think there's been some kind of mistake. This can't be right.
What are you talking about?

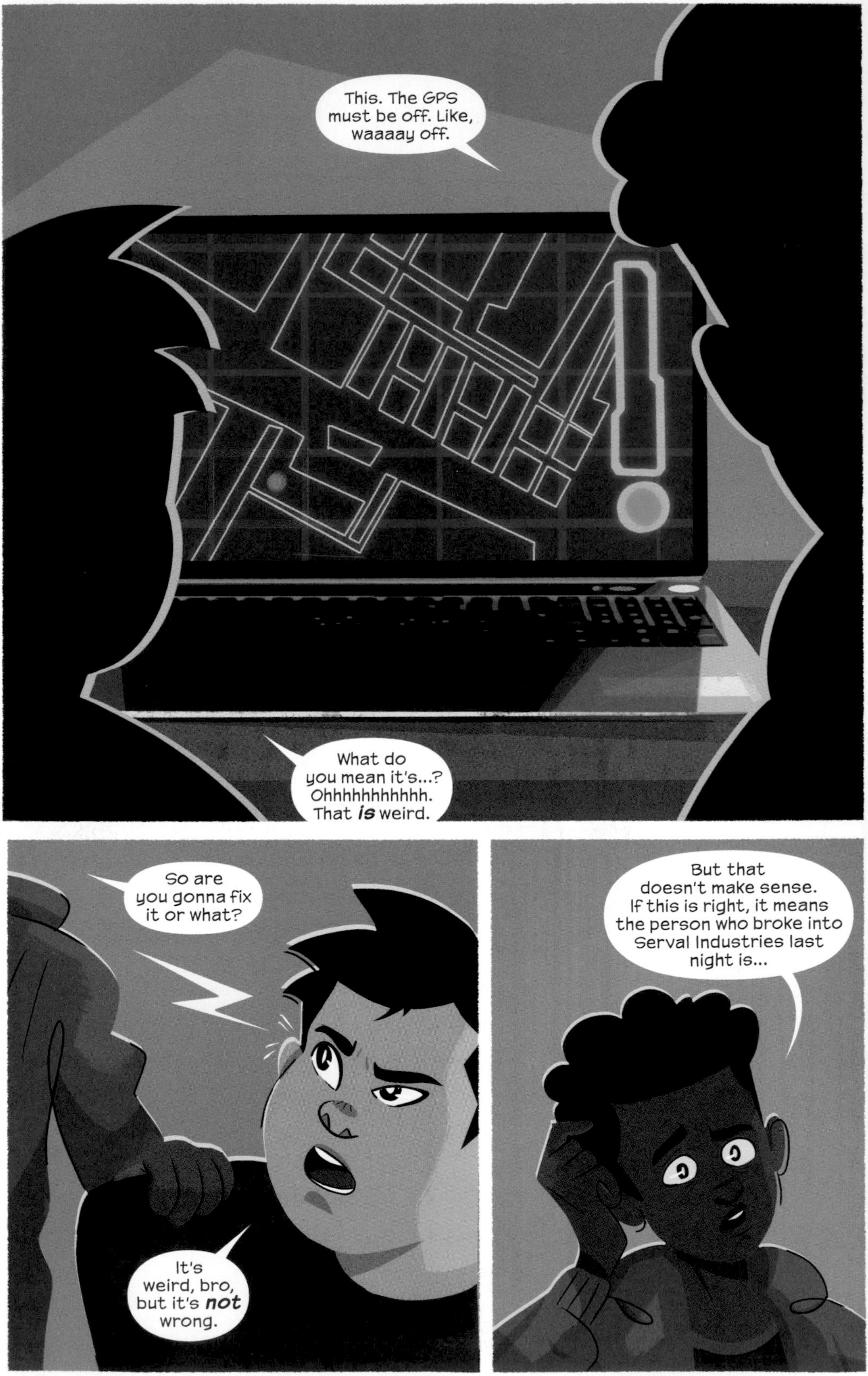
This. The GPS must be off. Like, waaaay off.
What do you mean it's...? Ohhhhhhhhhhh. That *is* weird.
So are you gonna fix it or what?
It's weird, bro, but it's *not* wrong.
But that doesn't make sense. If this is right, it means the person who broke into Serval Industries last night is...

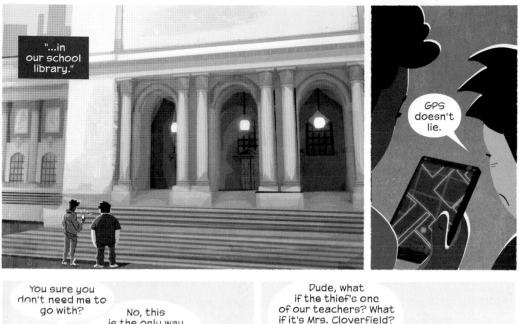

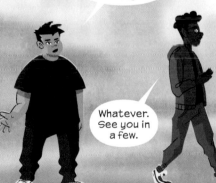

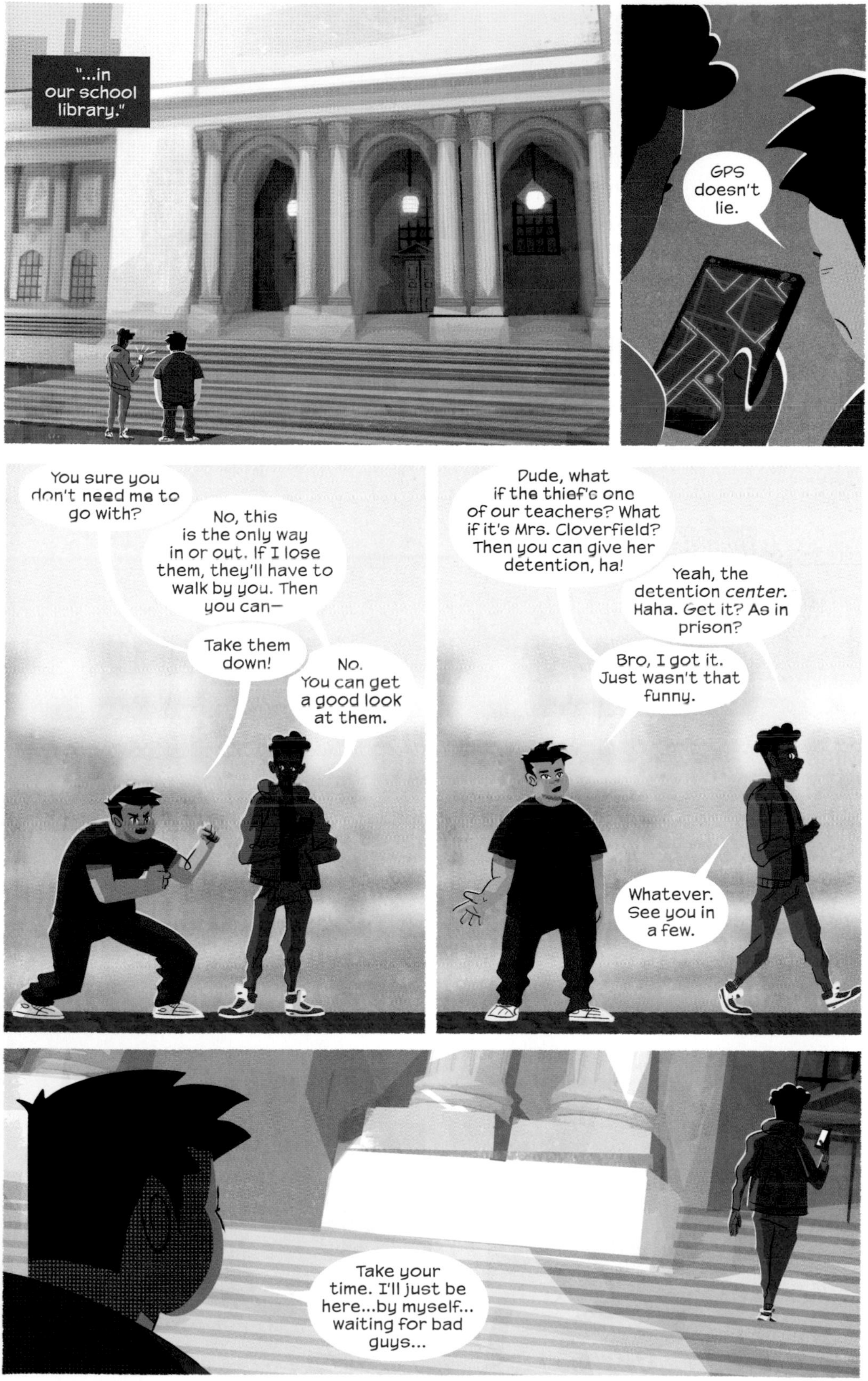
"...in our school library."
GPS doesn't lie.
You sure you don't need me to go with?
No, this is the only way in or out. If I lose them, they'll have to walk by you. Then you can—
Take them down!
No. You can get a good look at them.
Dude, what if the thief's one of our teachers? What if it's Mrs. Cloverfield? Then you can give her detention, ha!
Yeah, the detention *center.* Haha. Get it? As in prison?
Bro, I got it. Just wasn't that funny.
Whatever. See you in a few.
Take your time. I'll just be here...by myself... waiting for bad guys...

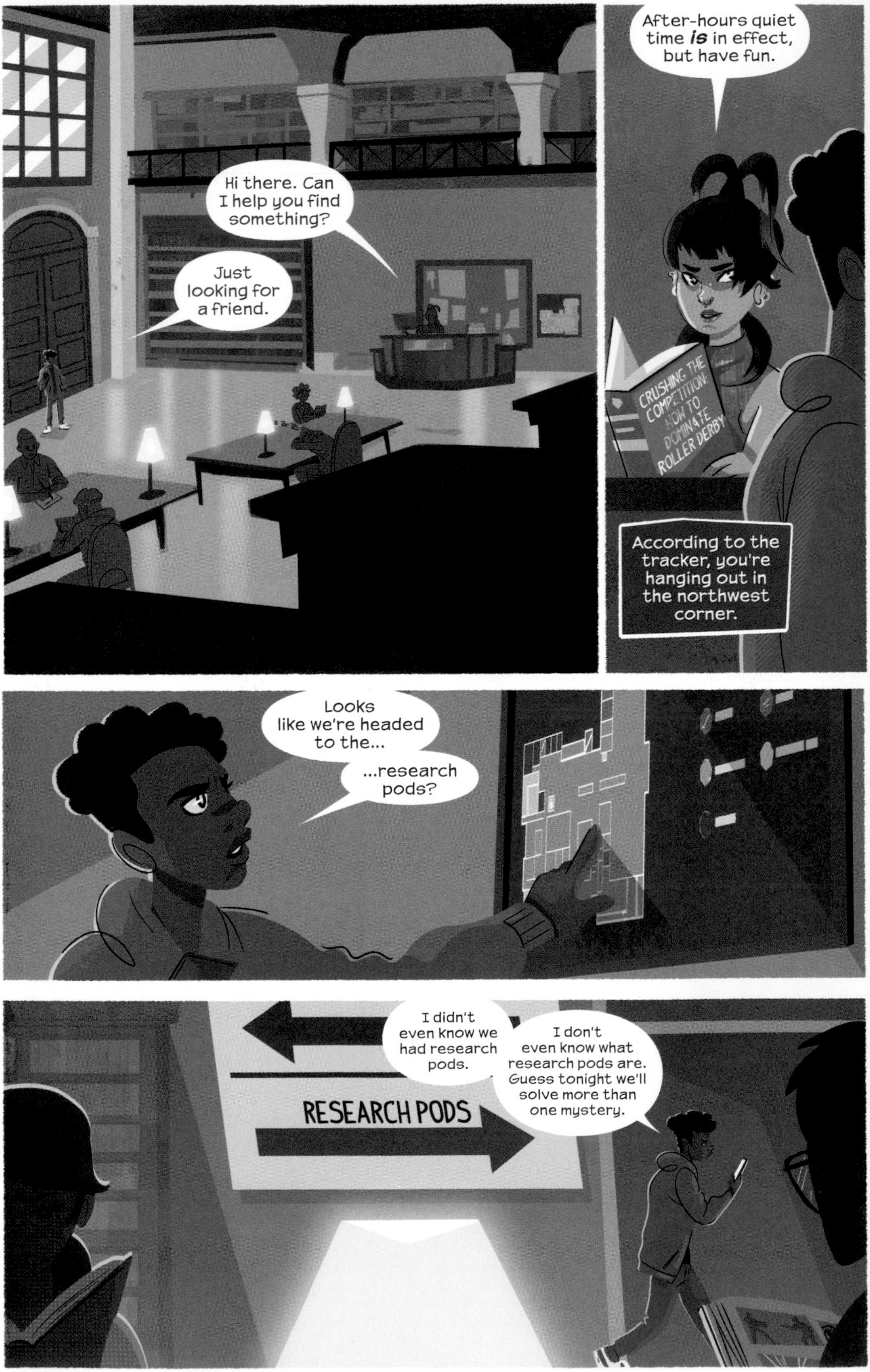
Hi there. Can I help you find something?
Just looking for a friend.
After-hours quiet time *is* in effect, but have fun.
CRUSHING THE COMPETITION: HOW TO DOMINATE ROLLER DERBY
According to the tracker, you're hanging out in the northwest corner.
Looks like we're headed to the...
...research pods?
RESEARCH PODS
I didn't even know we had research pods.
I don't even know what research pods are. Guess tonight we'll solve more than one mystery.

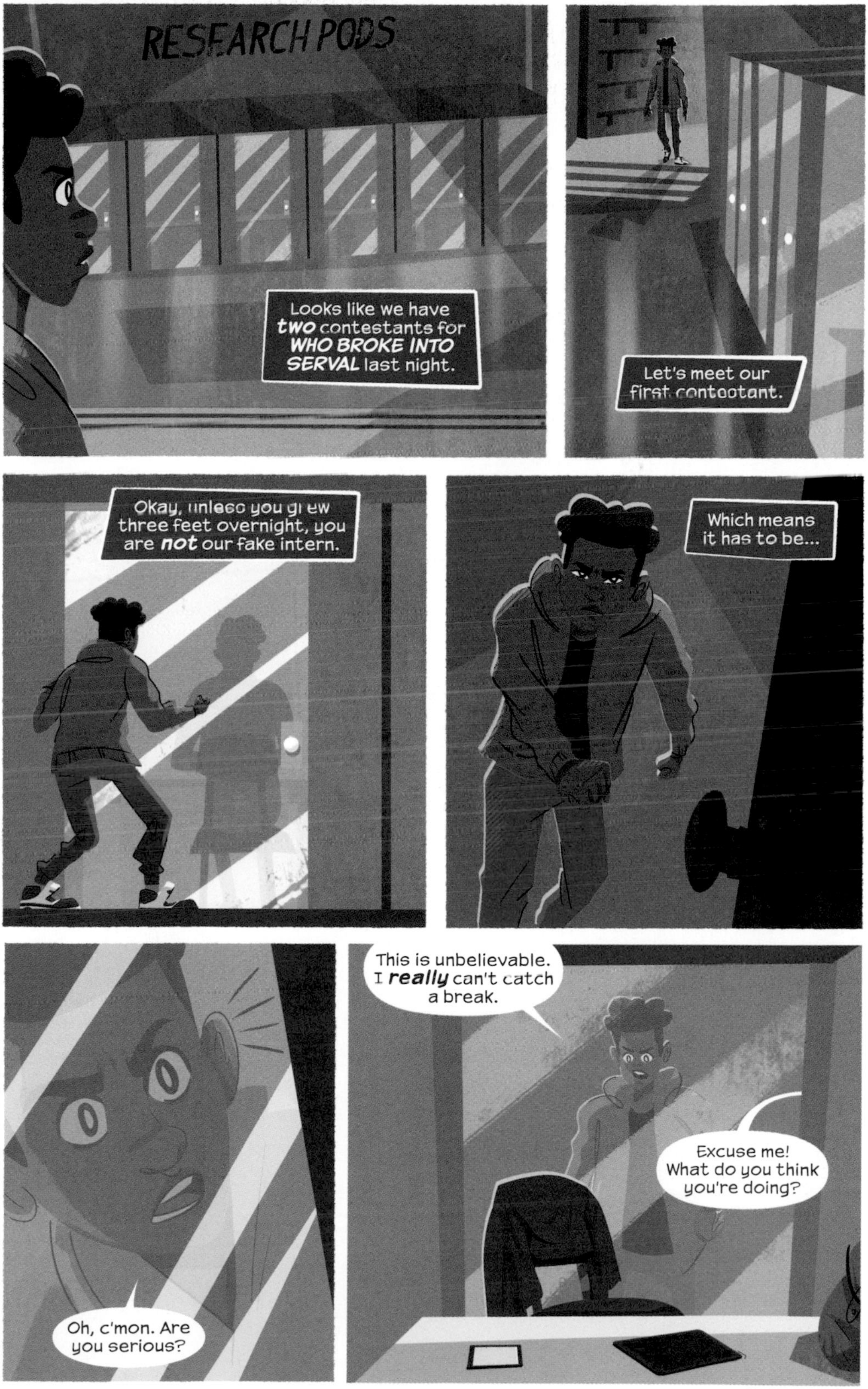
RESEARCH PODS
Looks like we have **two** contestants for **WHO BROKE INTO SERVAL** last night.
Let's meet our first contestant.
Okay, unless you grew three feet overnight, you are **not** our fake intern.
Which means it has to be...
Oh, c'mon. Are you serious?
This is unbelievable. I **really** can't catch a break.
Excuse me! What do you think you're doing?

A short while later.

Maybe it's what they might lose.

Okay, but why would Kyle break into Serval?

One day I'd love to discuss the fact that you get to do all the fun stuff.

Because she's searching for her dad.

Aww, Ganke, I'd be lost without your awesome techie brain.

So she thinks Serval disappeared her dad? Why? What would they gain?

THWIP

You're just saying that.

This tracking app that you recalibrated is pretty dope.

Actually, I completely redesigned it.

See? You're a tech god. But, uh, looks like Kyle's on the move, so.

Text me when you're on your way home? I worry.

74

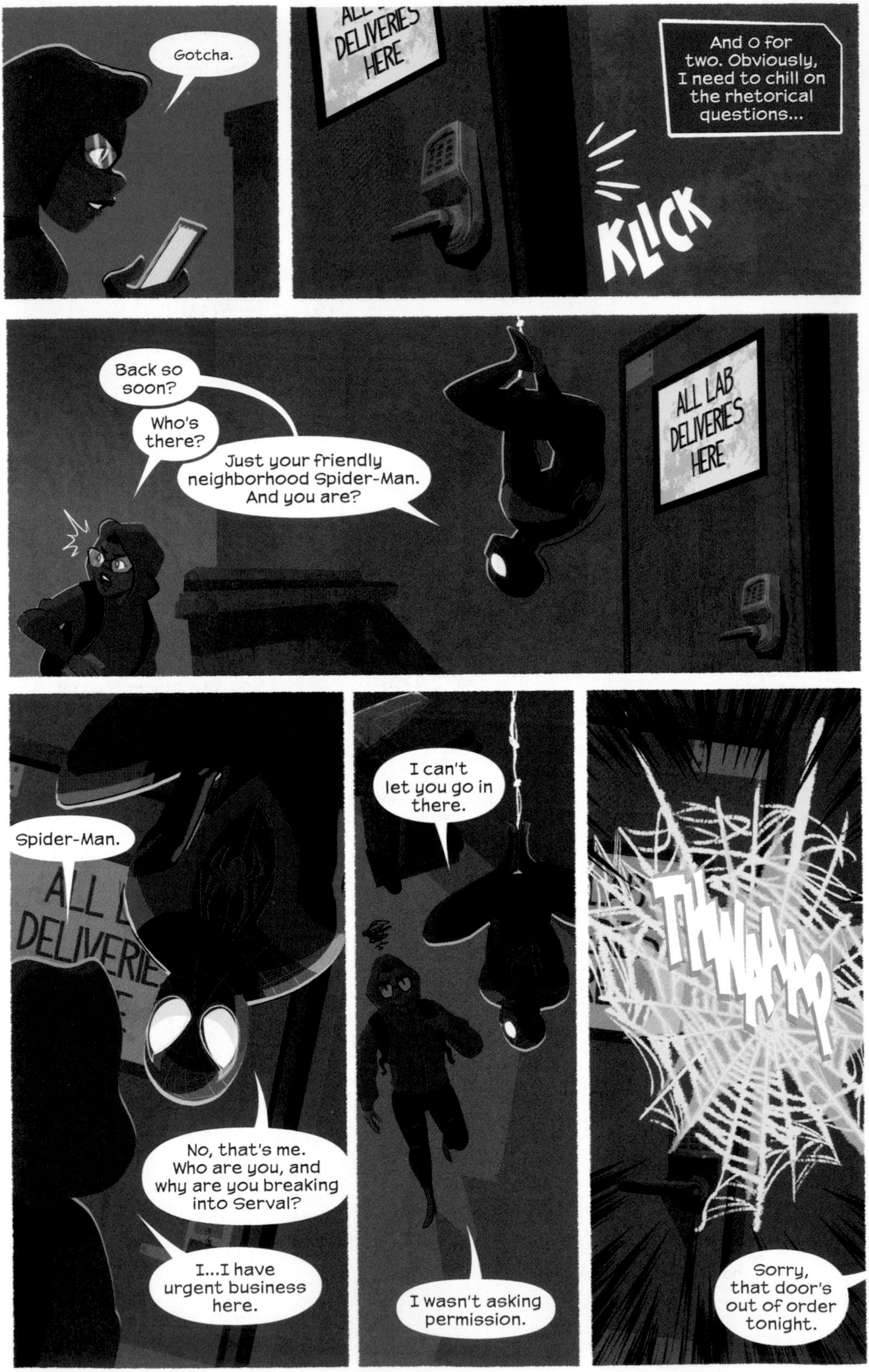
Gotcha.
ALL DELIVERIES HERE
And 0 for two. Obviously, I need to chill on the rhetorical questions...
KLICK
Back so soon?
Who's there?
Just your friendly neighborhood Spider-Man. And you are?
ALL LAB DELIVERIES HERE
Spider-Man.
No, that's me. Who are you, and why are you breaking into Serval?
I...I have urgent business here.
I can't let you go in there.
I wasn't asking permission.
THWAAAP
Sorry, that door's out of order tonight.

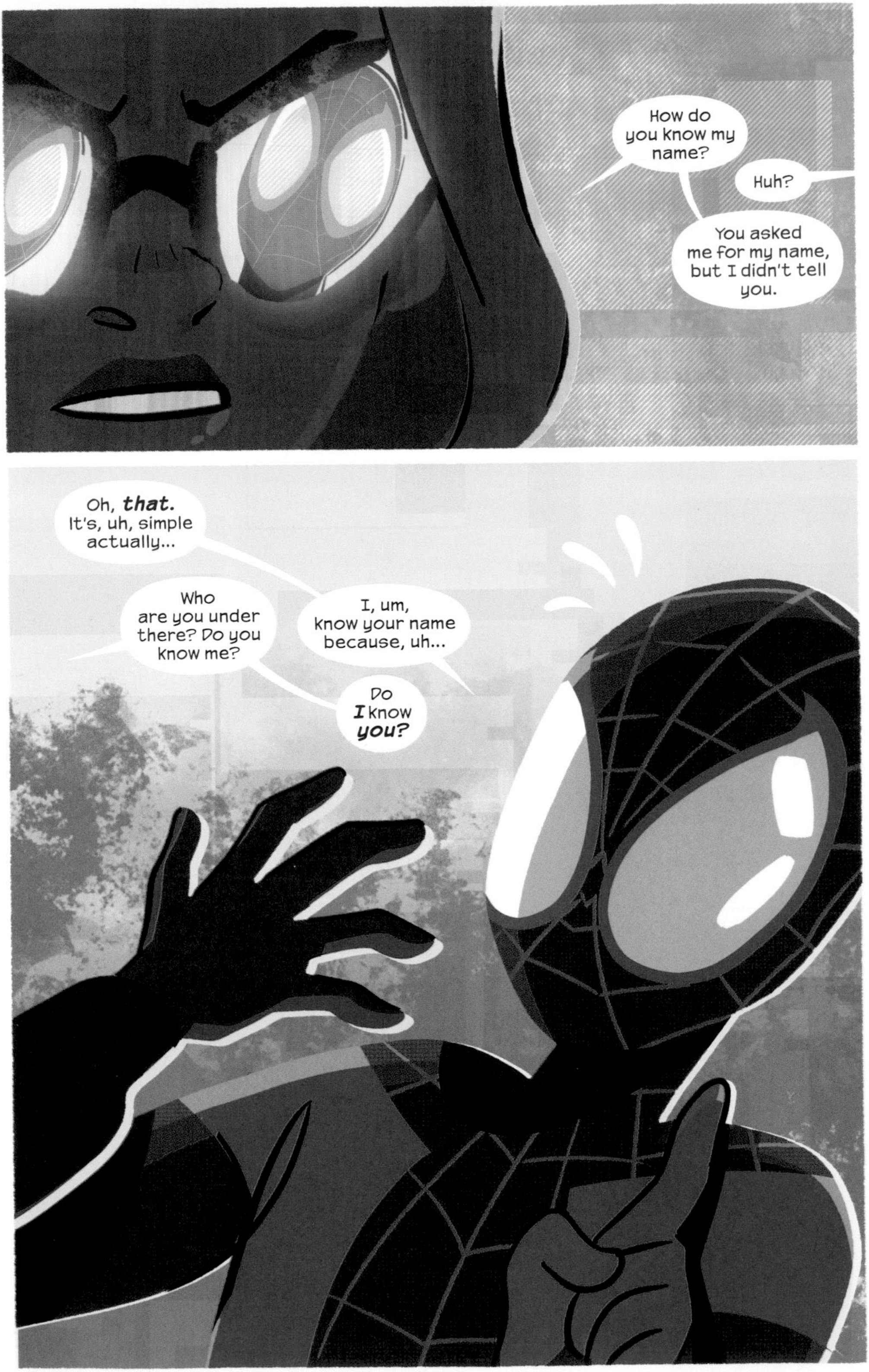
How do you know my name?
Huh?
You asked me for my name, but I didn't tell you.
Oh, ***that.*** It's, uh, simple actually...
I, um, know your name because, uh...
Who are you under there? Do you know me?
Do ***I*** know ***you?***

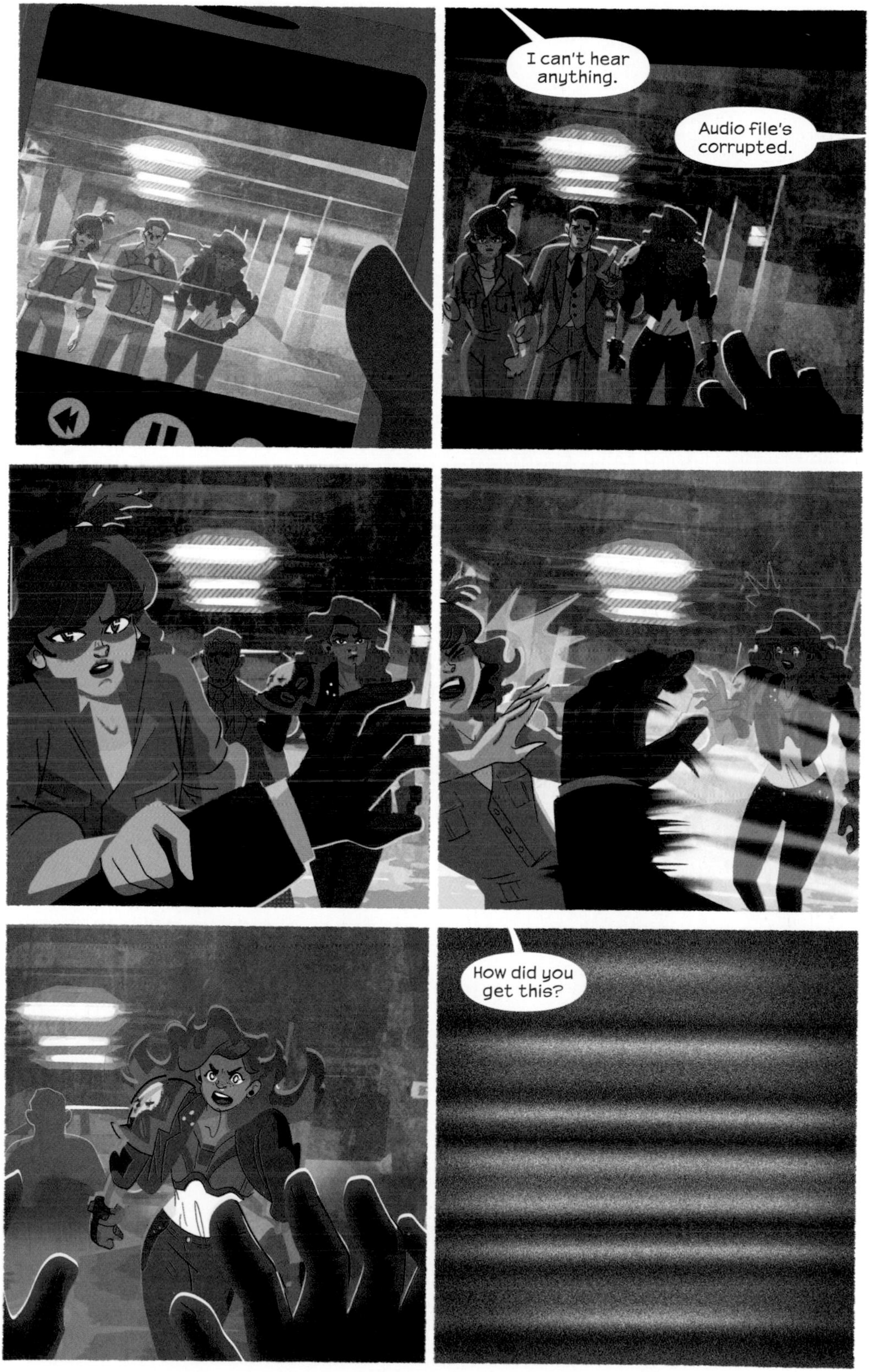
I can't hear anything.
Audio file's corrupted.
How did you get this?

CHAPTER

FIVE

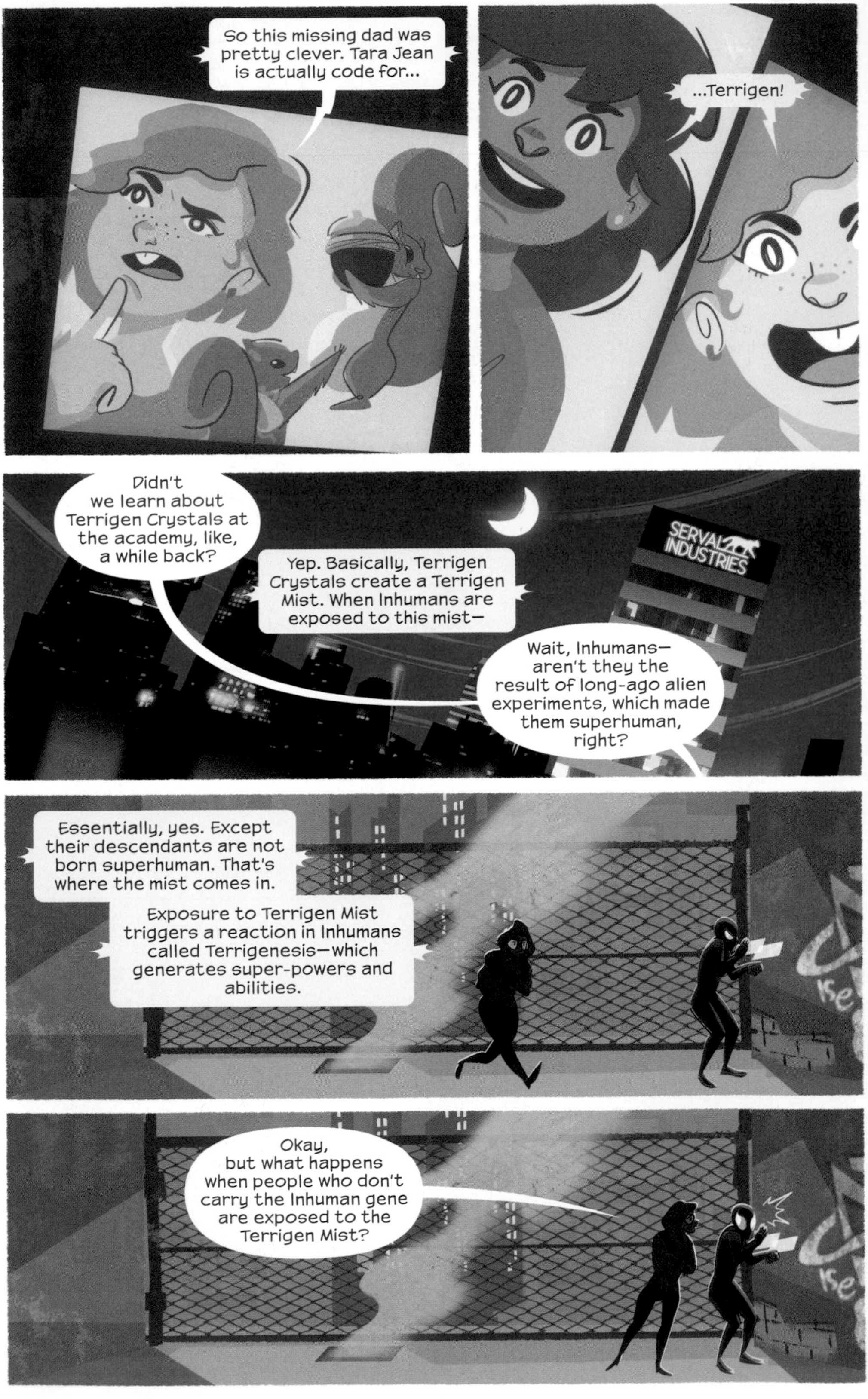
So this missing dad was pretty clever. Tara Jean is actually code for...
...Terrigen!
Didn't we learn about Terrigen Crystals at the academy, like, a while back?
SERVAL INDUSTRIES
Yep. Basically, Terrigen Crystals create a Terrigen Mist. When Inhumans are exposed to this mist—
Wait, Inhumans— aren't they the result of long-ago alien experiments, which made them superhuman, right?
Essentially, yes. Except their descendants are not born superhuman. That's where the mist comes in.
Exposure to Terrigen Mist triggers a reaction in Inhumans called Terrigenesis—which generates super-powers and abilities.
Okay, but what happens when people who don't carry the Inhuman gene are exposed to the Terrigen Mist?

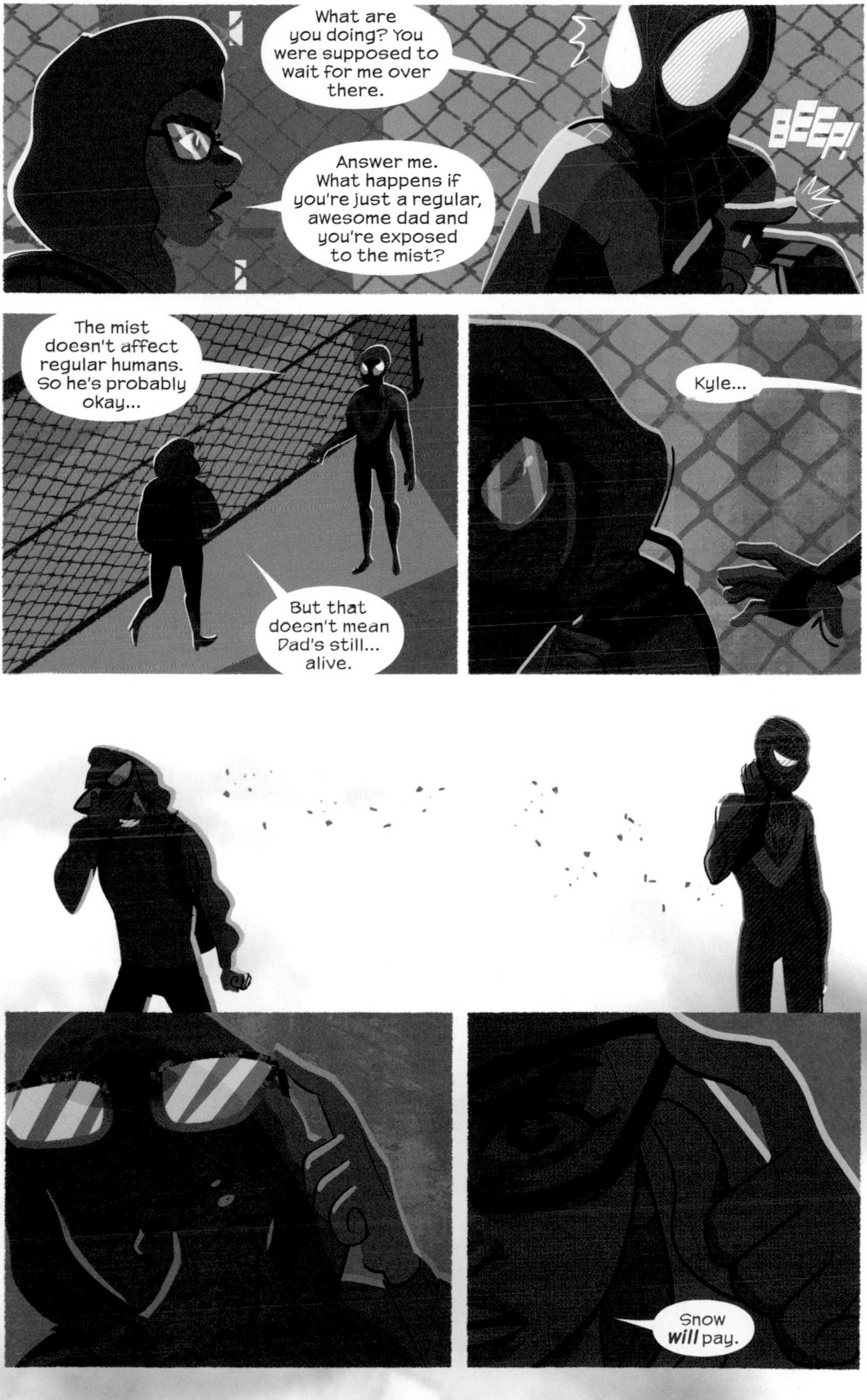
What are you doing? You were supposed to wait for me over there.
BEEP!
Answer me. What happens if you're just a regular, awesome dad and you're exposed to the mist?
The mist doesn't affect regular humans. So he's probably okay...
But that doesn't mean Dad's still... alive.
Kyle...
Snow *will* pay.

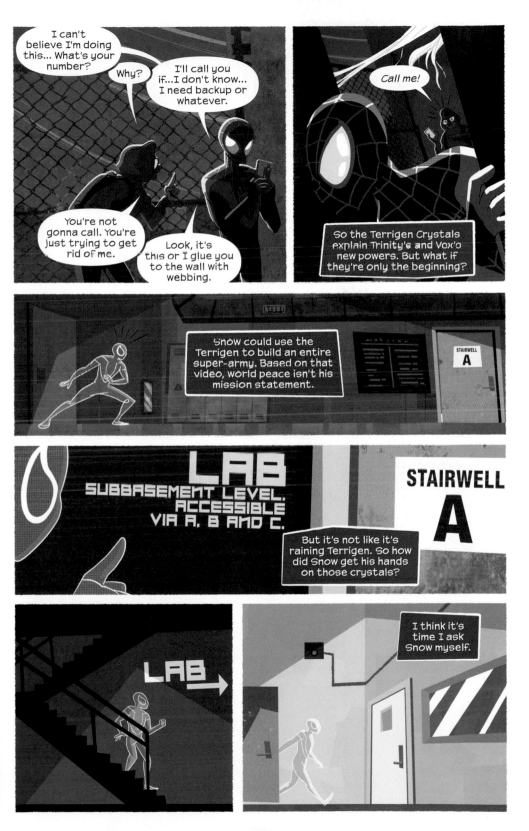

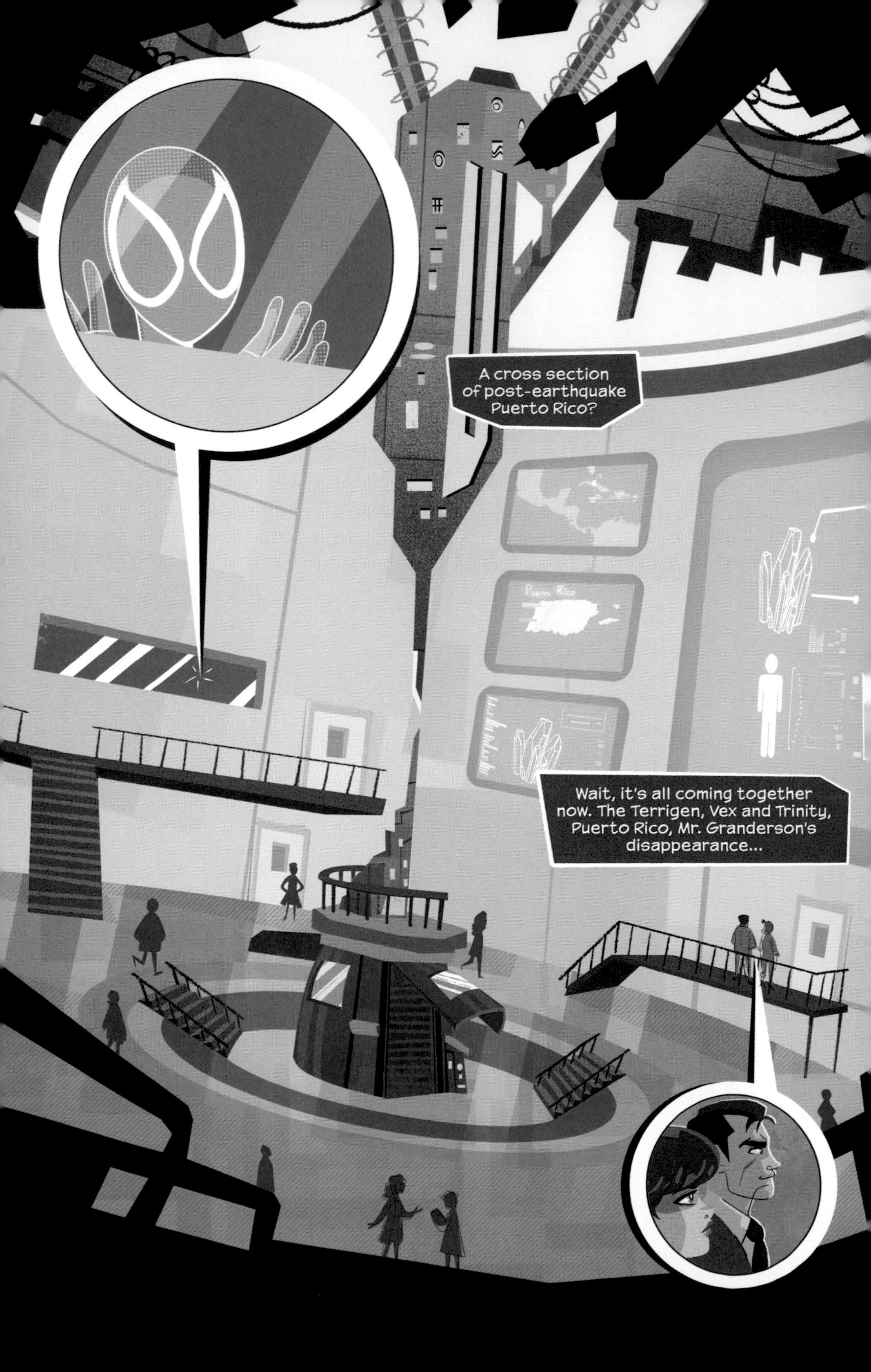
A cross section of post-earthquake Puerto Rico?
Puerto Rico
Wait, it's all coming together now. The Terrigen, Vex and Trinity, Puerto Rico, Mr. Granderson's disappearance...

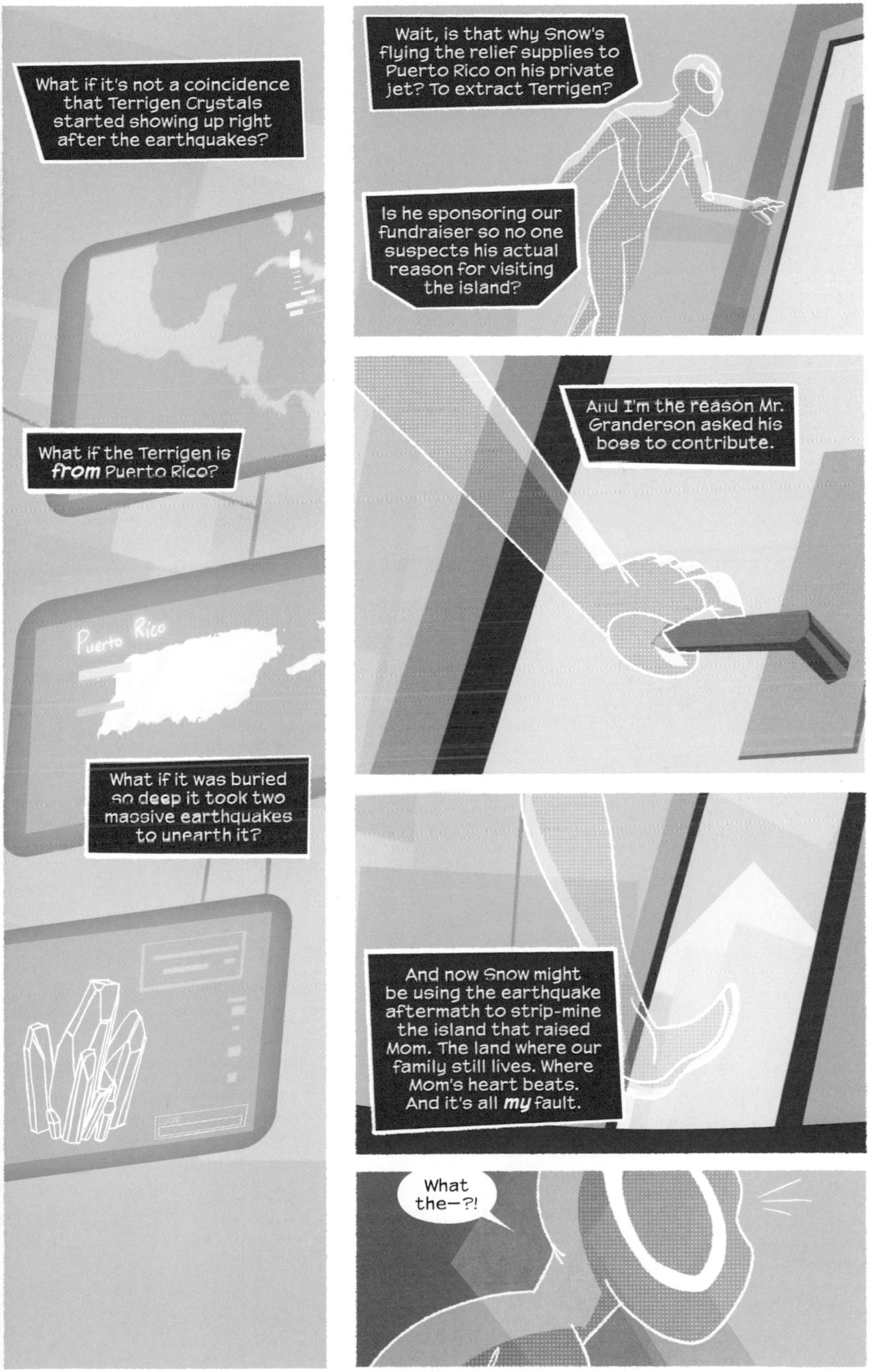

What if it's not a coincidence that Terrigen Crystals started showing up right after the earthquakes?

Wait, is that why Snow's flying the relief supplies to Puerto Rico on his private jet? To extract Terrigen?

Is he sponsoring our fundraiser so no one suspects his actual reason for visiting the island?

What if the Terrigen is *from* Puerto Rico?

And I'm the reason Mr. Granderson asked his boss to contribute.

What if it was buried so deep it took two massive earthquakes to unearth it?

And now Snow might be using the earthquake aftermath to strip-mine the island that raised Mom. The land where our family still lives. Where Mom's heart beats. And it's all *my* fault.

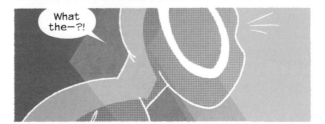

What the—?!

Puerto Rico

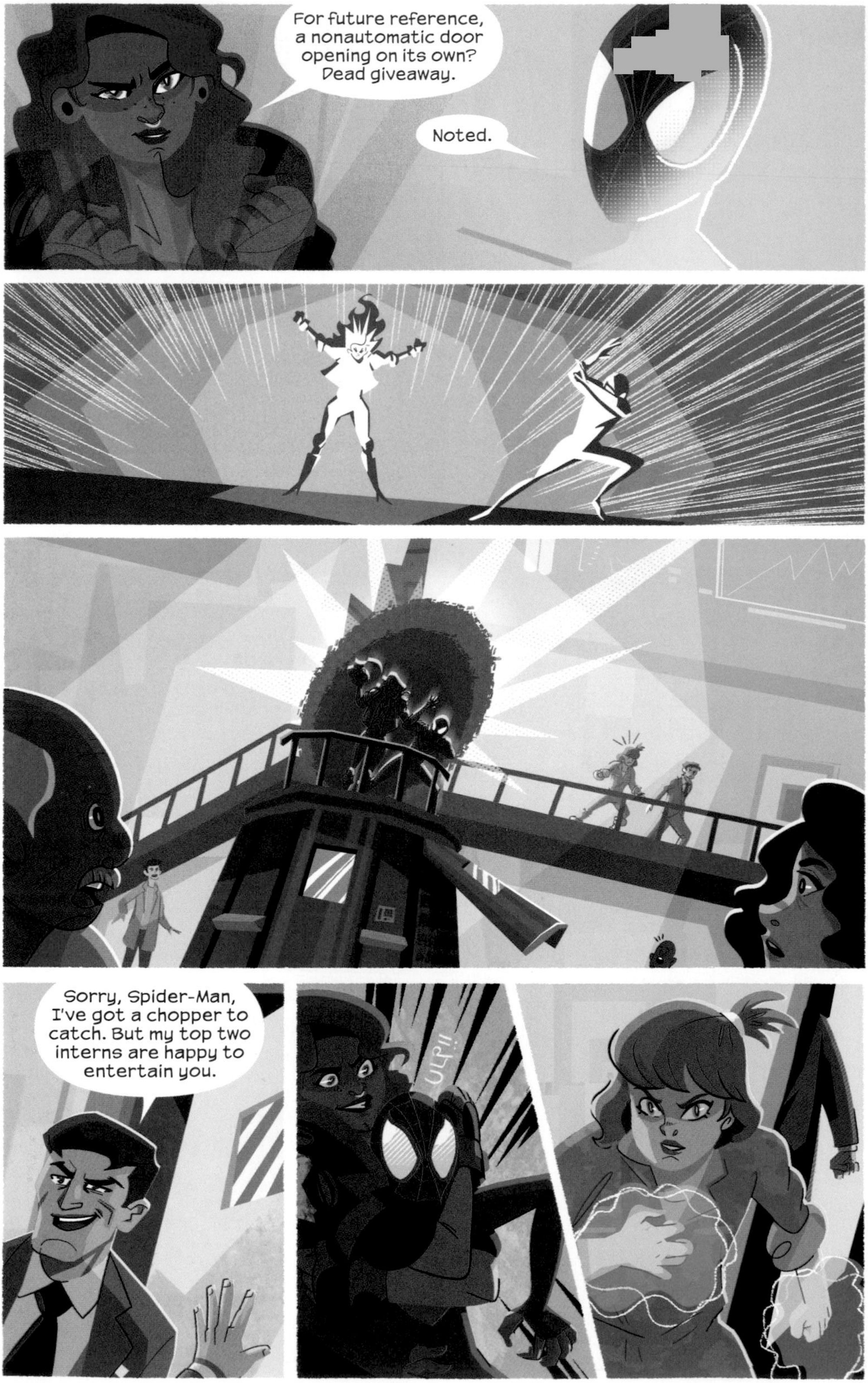
For future reference, a nonautomatic door opening on its own? Dead giveaway.
Noted.
Sorry, Spider-Man, I've got a chopper to catch. But my top two interns are happy to entertain you.
ULP!!

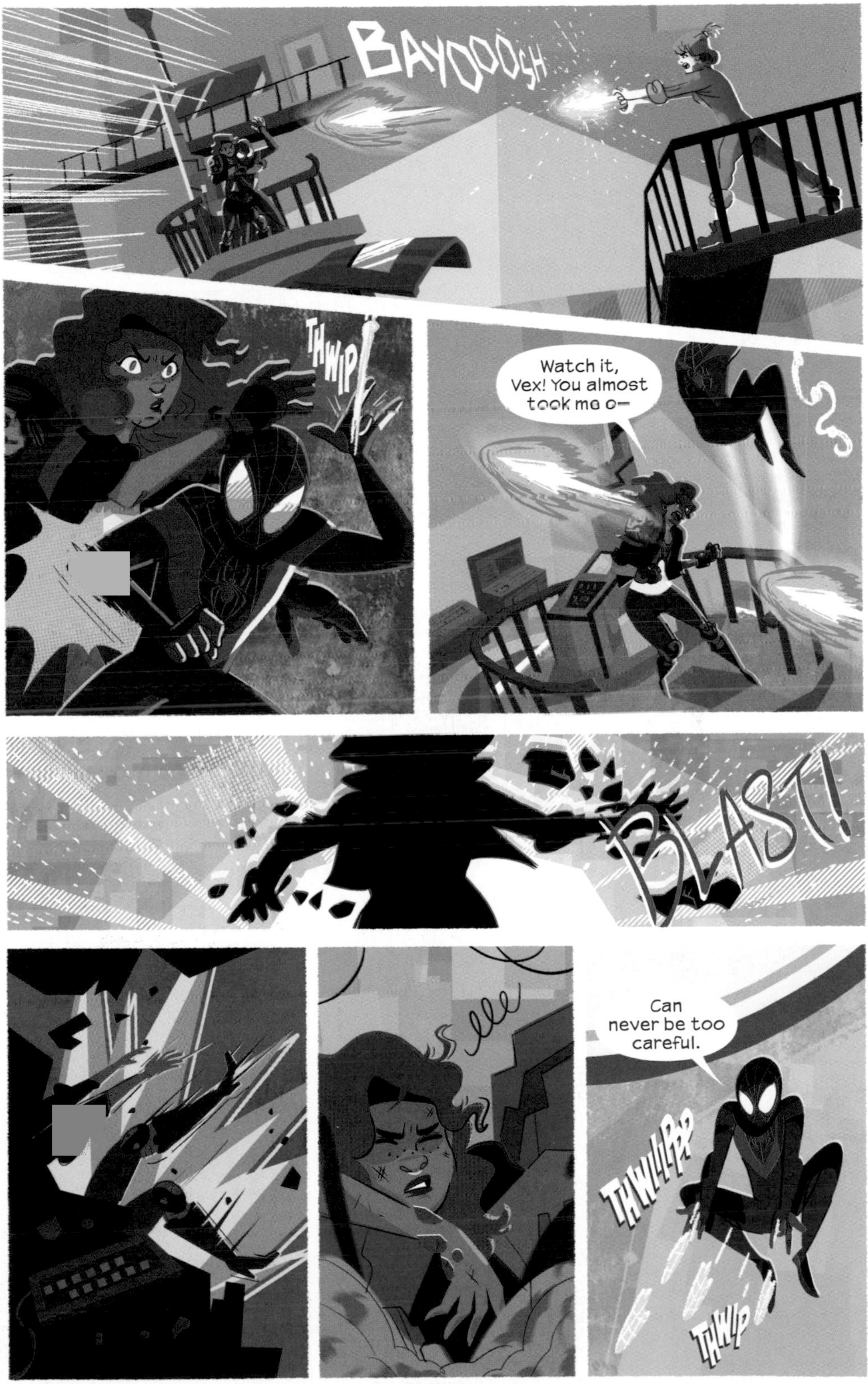
BAYOOOSH
THWIP
Watch it, Vex! You almost took me o—
BLAST!
Can never be too careful.
THWLLLPPP
THWIP

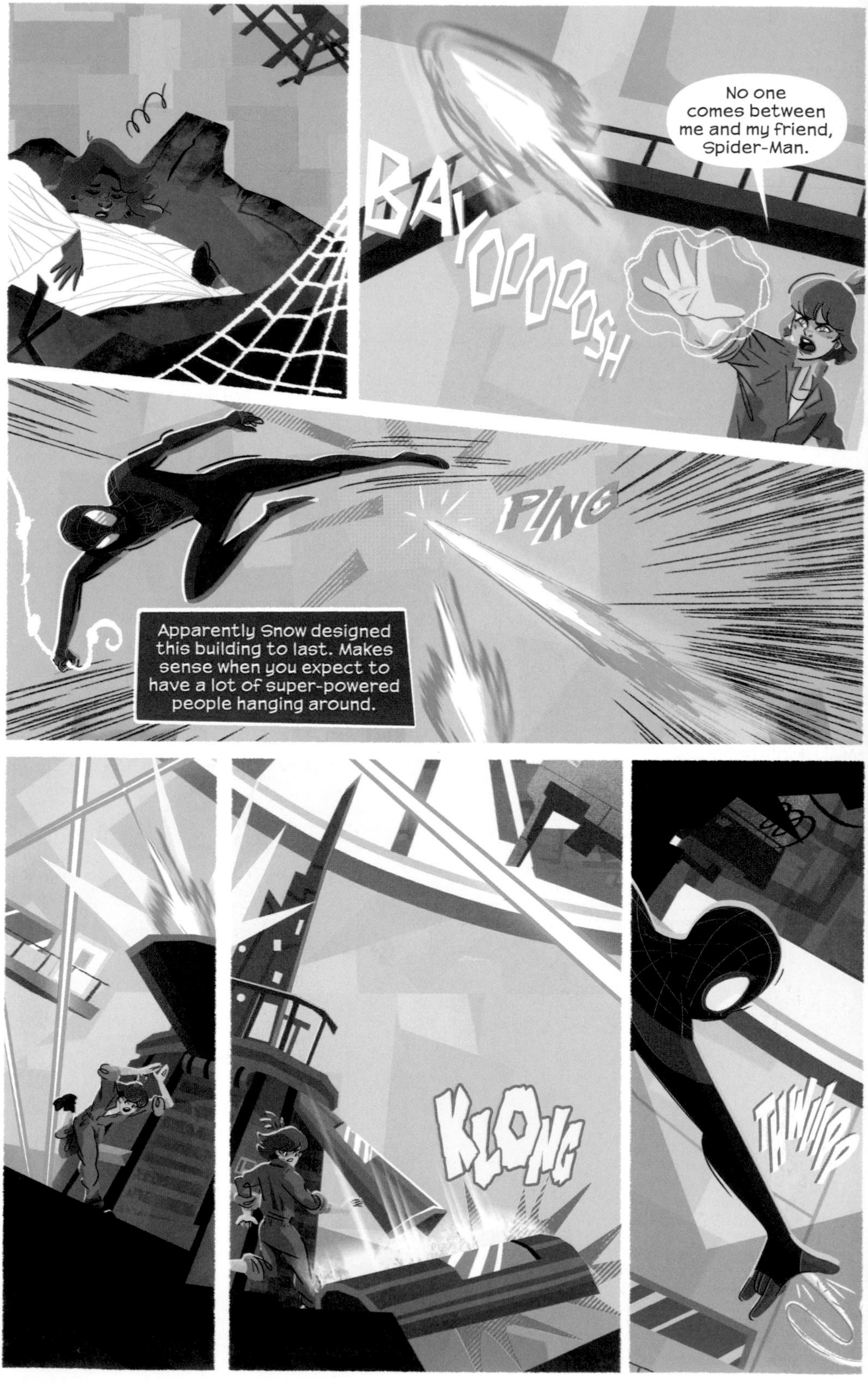
BAYOOOOOSH
No one comes between me and my friend, Spider-Man.
PING
Apparently Snow designed this building to last. Makes sense when you expect to have a lot of super-powered people hanging around.
KLONG
THWIP

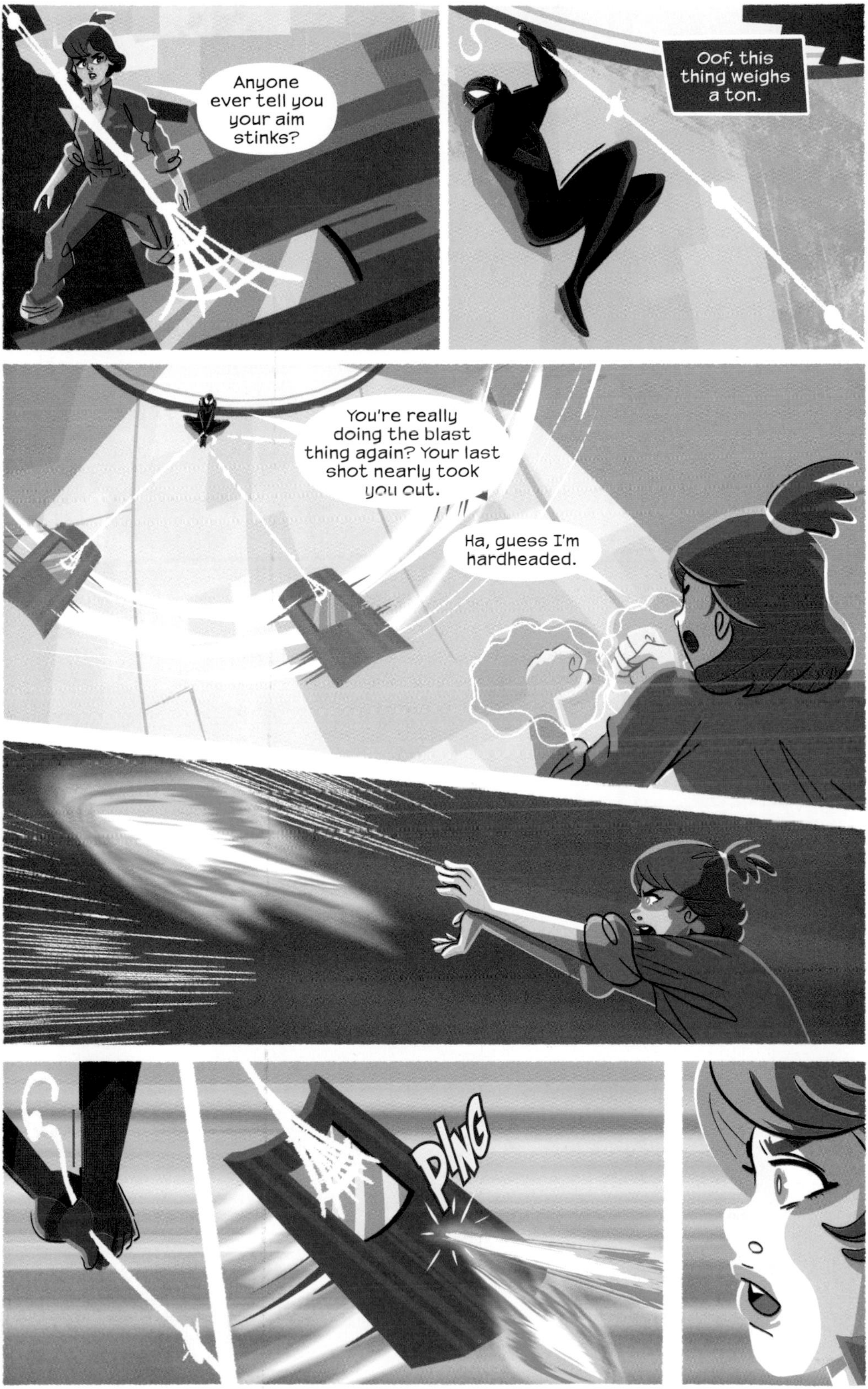
Anyone ever tell you your aim stinks?
Oof, this thing weighs a ton.
You're really doing the blast thing again? Your last shot nearly took you out.
Ha, guess I'm hardheaded.
PING

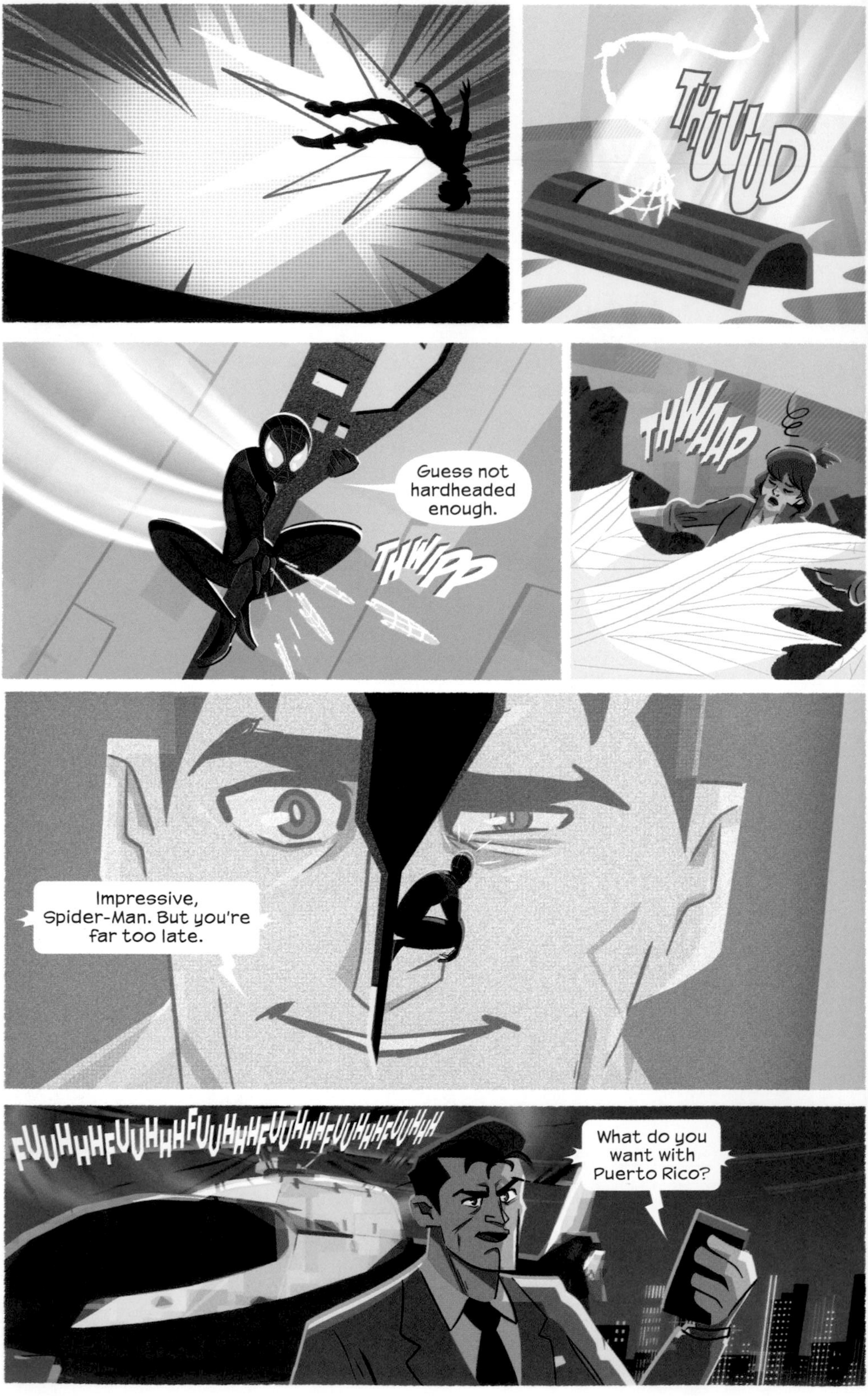
THUUUD
Guess not hardheaded enough.
THWIPP
THWAAP
Impressive, Spider-Man. But you're far too late.
FUUHHHFUUHHHFUUHHHFUUHHHFUUHHHFUUHHH
What do you want with Puerto Rico?

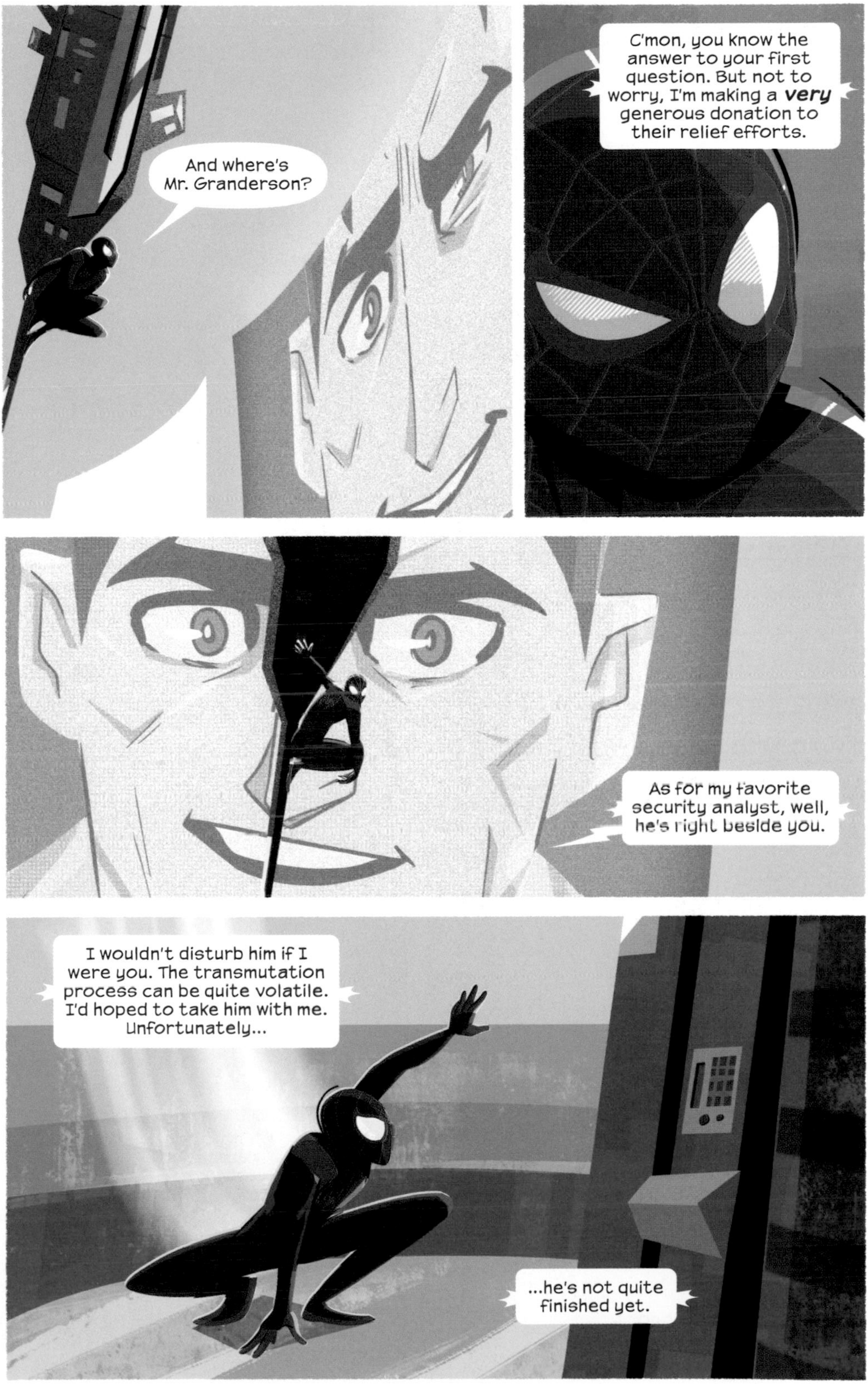
And where's Mr. Granderson?
C'mon, you know the answer to your first question. But not to worry, I'm making a **very** generous donation to their relief efforts.
As for my favorite security analyst, well, he's right beside you.
I wouldn't disturb him if I were you. The transmutation process can be quite volatile. I'd hoped to take him with me. Unfortunately...
...he's not quite finished yet.

CHAPTER
SIX

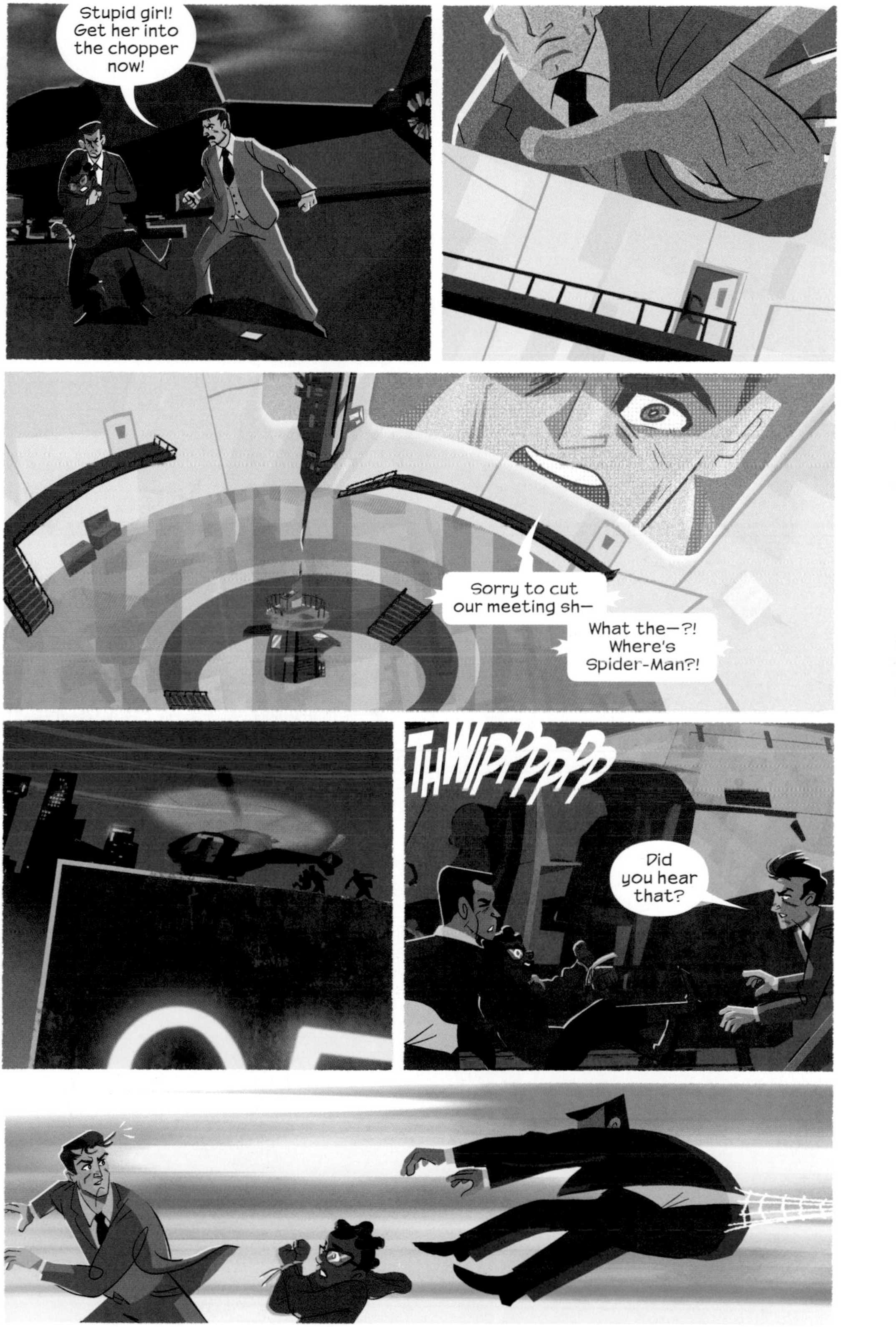
Stupid girl! Get her into the chopper now!
Sorry to cut our meeting sh—
What the—?! Where's Spider-Man?!
THWIPPPPPP
Did you hear that?

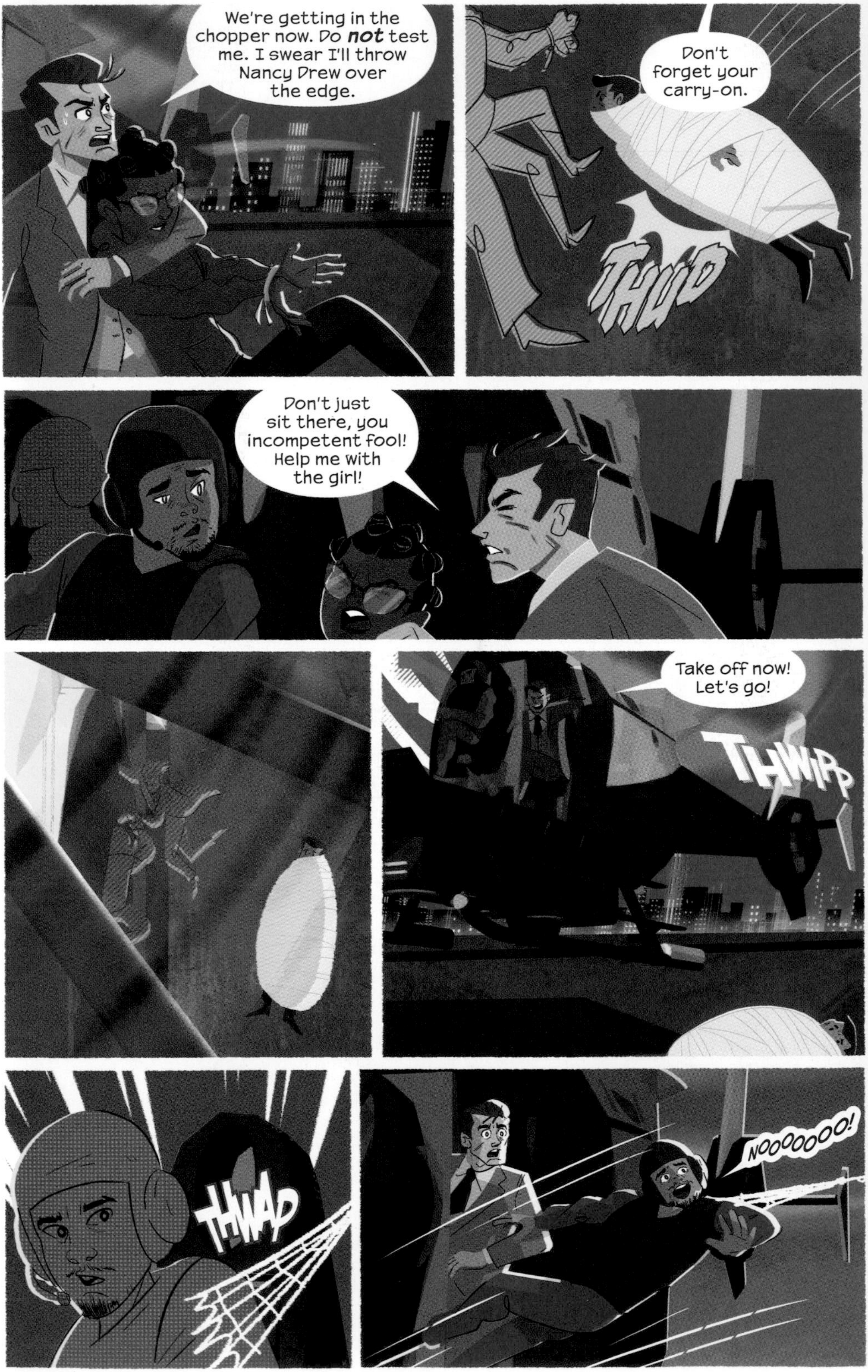
We're getting in the chopper now. Do **not** test me. I swear I'll throw Nancy Drew over the edge.
Don't forget your carry-on.
THUD
Don't just sit there, you incompetent fool! Help me with the girl!
Take off now! Let's go!
THWIPP
THWAP
NOOOOOOO!

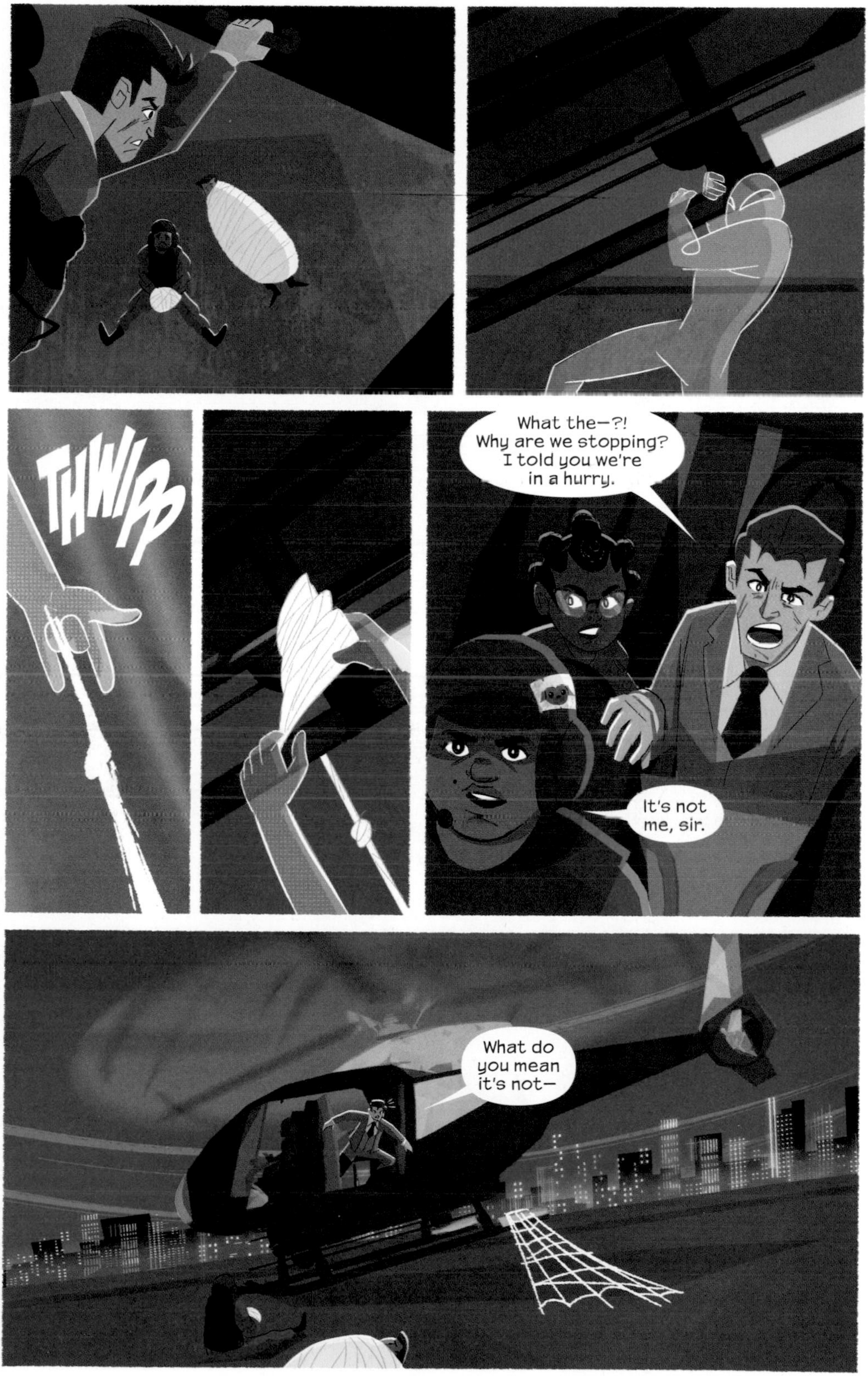
THWIPP
What the—?!
Why are we stopping?
I told you we're
in a hurry.
It's not
me, sir.
What do
you mean
it's not—

WOOOSH

Geoffo's Coffee

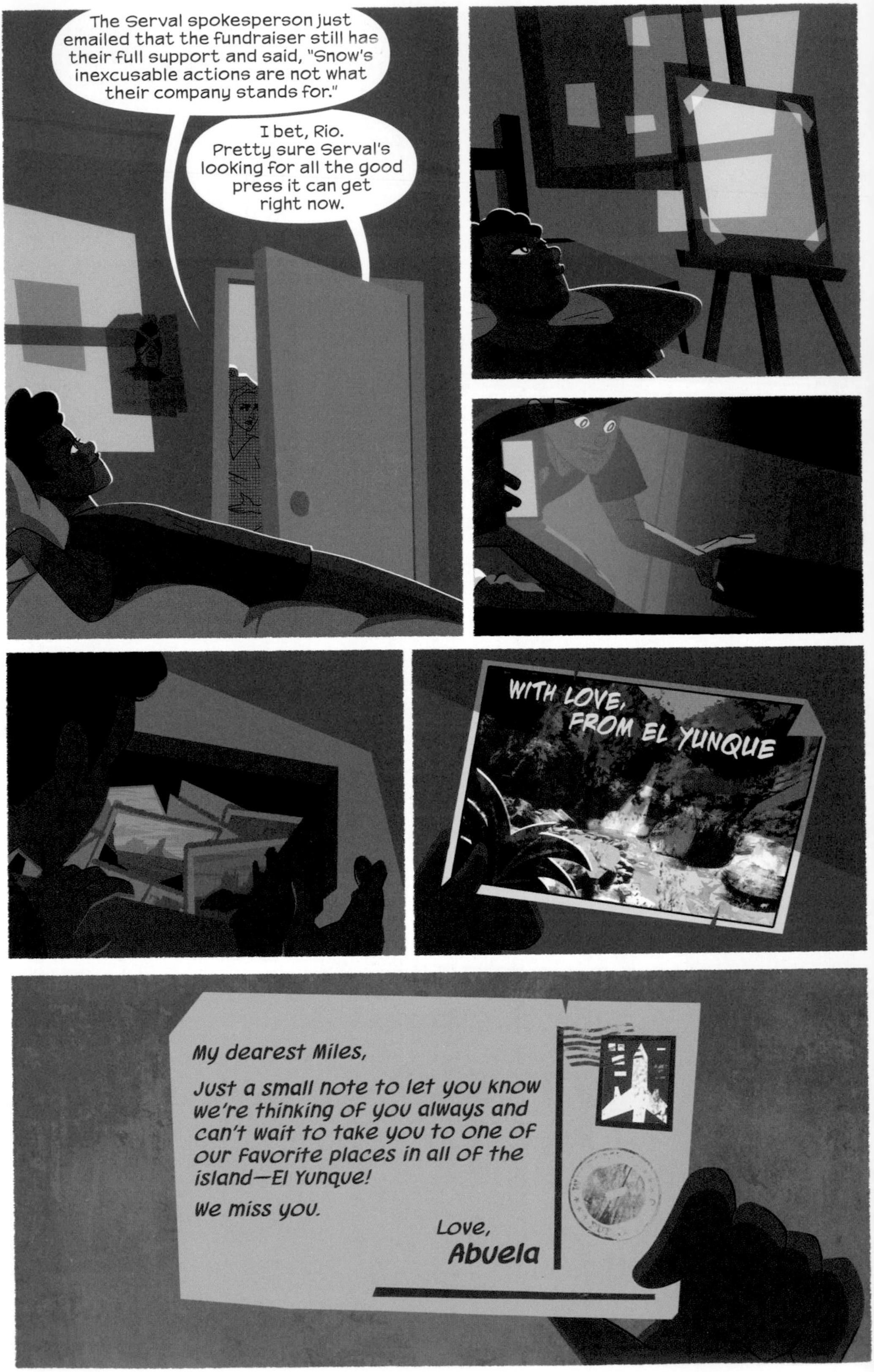

My dearest Miles,

Just a small note to let you know we're thinking of you always and can't wait to take you to one of our favorite places in all of the island—El Yunque!

We miss you.

Love,
Abuela

To every young super hero in the making,
the power is already within you.
—JR

To the future super heroes out there,
we need your uplifting stories more than ever.
—PL

JUSTIN A. REYNOLDS has always wanted to be a writer. *Opposite of Always*, his debut novel, was an Indies Introduce selection and a School Library Journal Best Book, has been translated into seventeen languages and is being developed for film with Paramount Players. His second novel, *Early Departures*, arrived September 2020. Justin hangs out in northeast Ohio with his family and likes it and is probably somewhere, right now, dancing terribly. You can find him at justinareynolds.com.

PABLO LEON is an artist and designer whose clients include Warner Brothers Animation, OddBot Inc., Puny Entertainment, Bento Box Entertainment, and more. His original comic story *The Journey*, about the true accounts of people migrating from Latin America to the United States, was a 2019 Eisner Award nominee. He lives in Los Angeles, California.

CHECK OUT A SNEAK PEEK OF

MS. MARVEL
STRETCHED THIN

COMING **FALL 2021!**

WRITTEN BY
NADIA SHAMMAS

ILLUSTRATED BY
NABI H. ALI

LAYOUTS BY
GEOFFO

LETTERS BY
VC's JOE CARAMAGNA

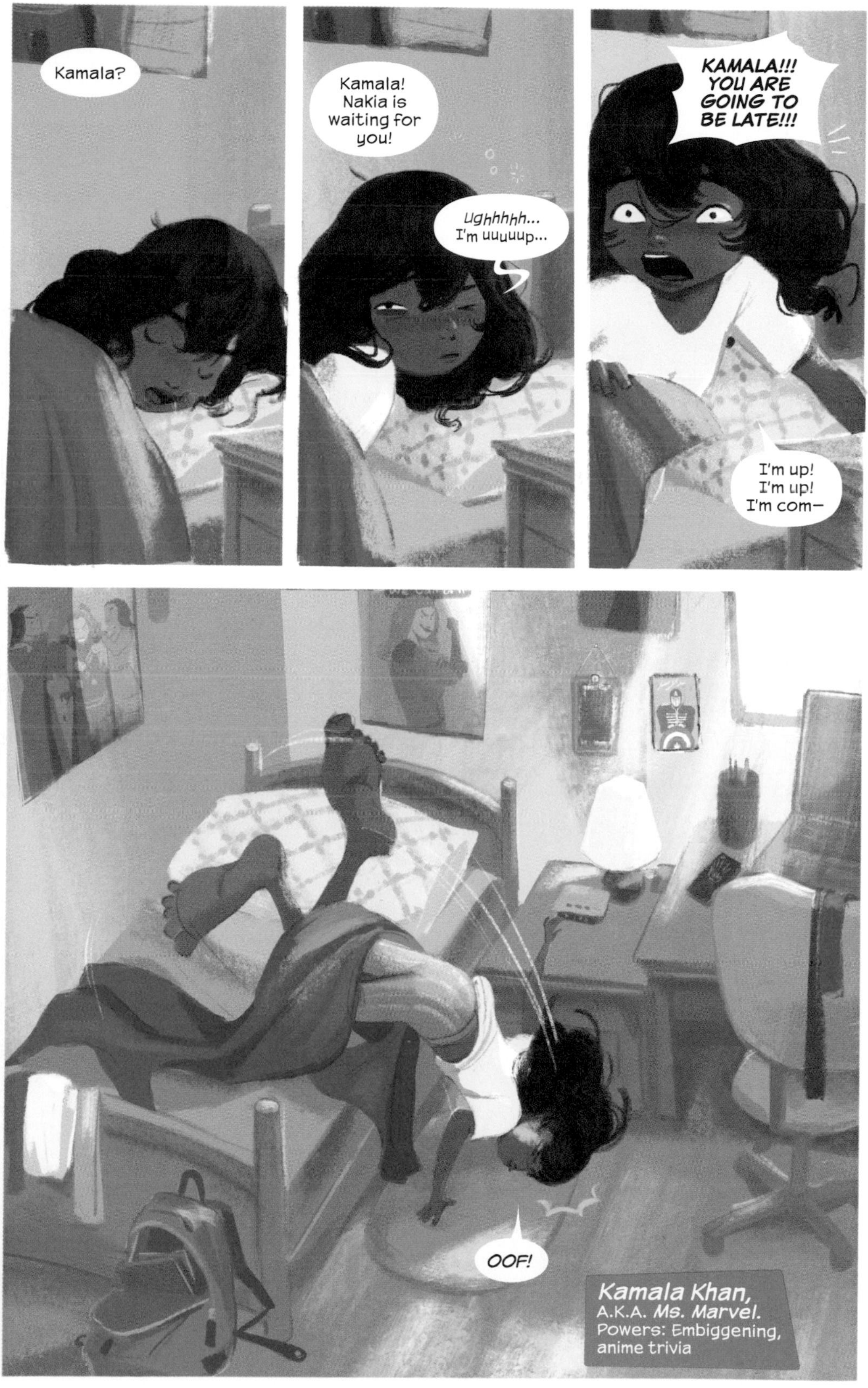
Kamala?
Kamala! Nakia is waiting for you!
Ughhhhh... I'm uuuuup...
KAMALA!!! YOU ARE GOING TO BE LATE!!!
I'm up! I'm up! I'm com—
OOF!
Kamala Khan, A.K.A. Ms. Marvel. Powers: Embiggening, anime trivia

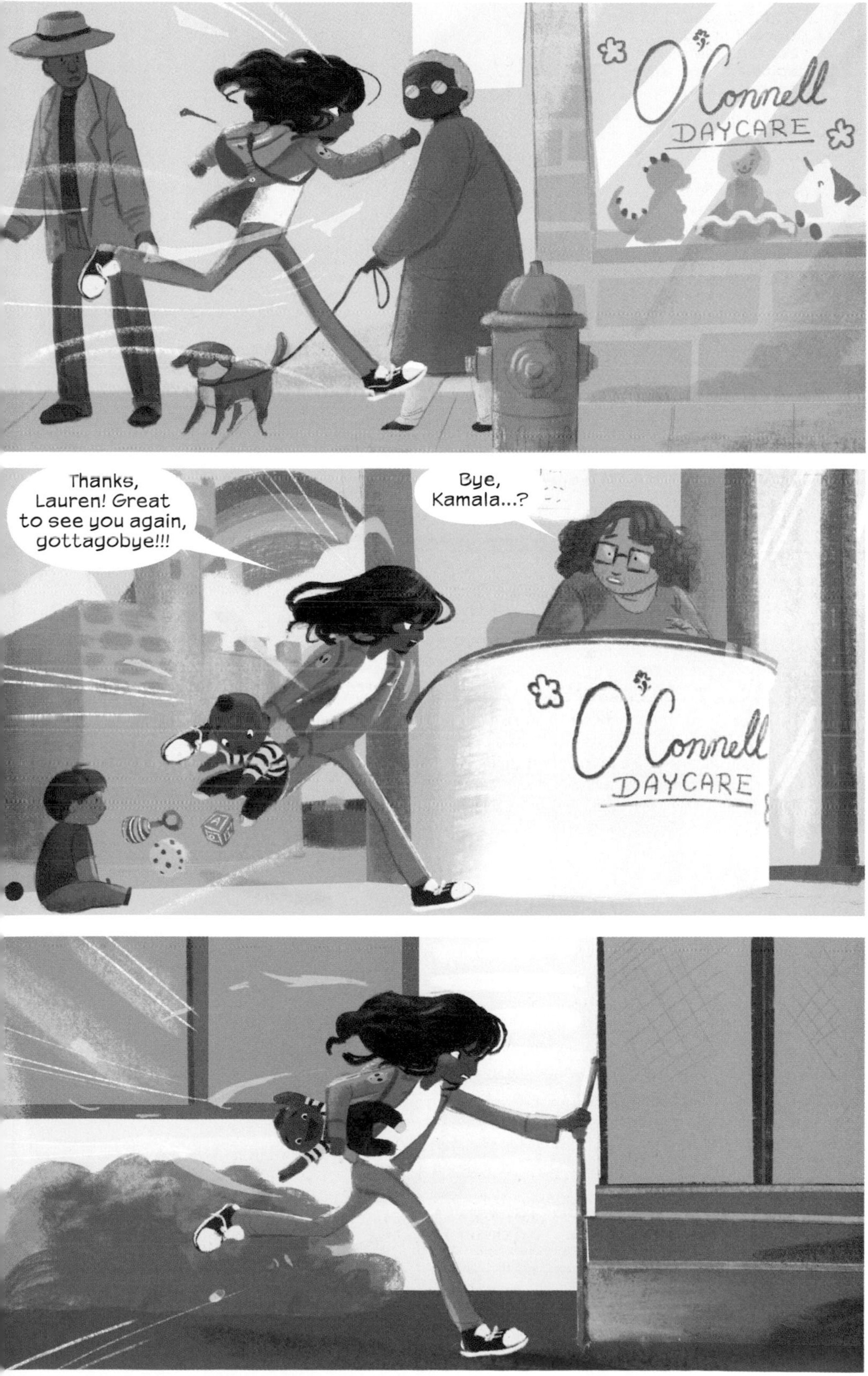
O'Connell
DAYCARE
Thanks, Lauren! Great to see you again, gottagobye!!!
Bye, Kamala...?
O'Connell
DAYCARE

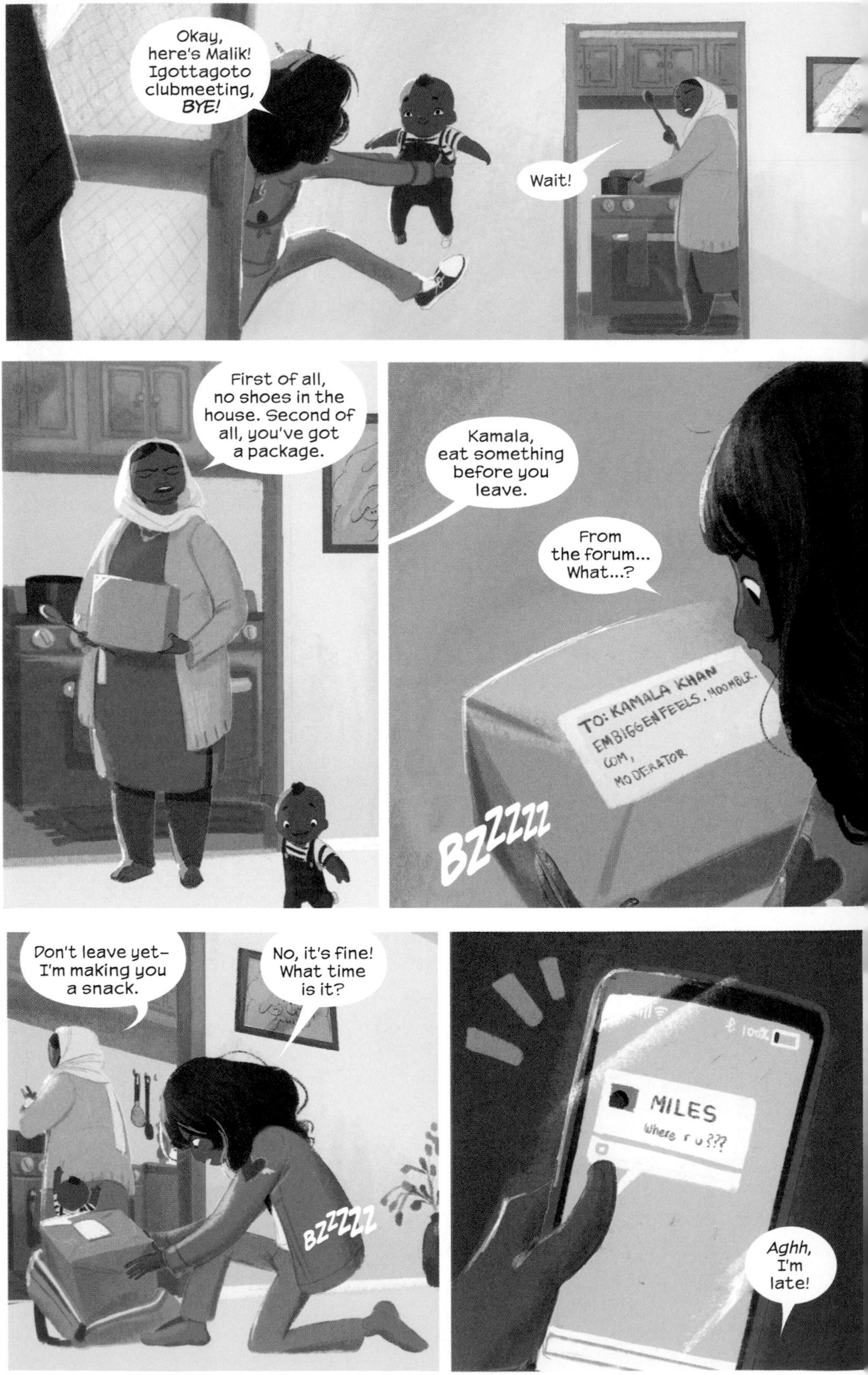
Okay, here's Malik! Igottagoto clubmeeting, *BYE!*
Wait!
First of all, no shoes in the house. Second of all, you've got a package.
Kamala, eat something before you leave.
From the forum... What...?
TO: KAMALA KHAN EMBIGGENFEELS.MOOMBLR.COM, MODERATOR
BZZZZZ
Don't leave yet– I'm making you a snack.
No, it's fine! What time is it?
BZZZZZ
MILES
Where r u???
Aghh, I'm late!

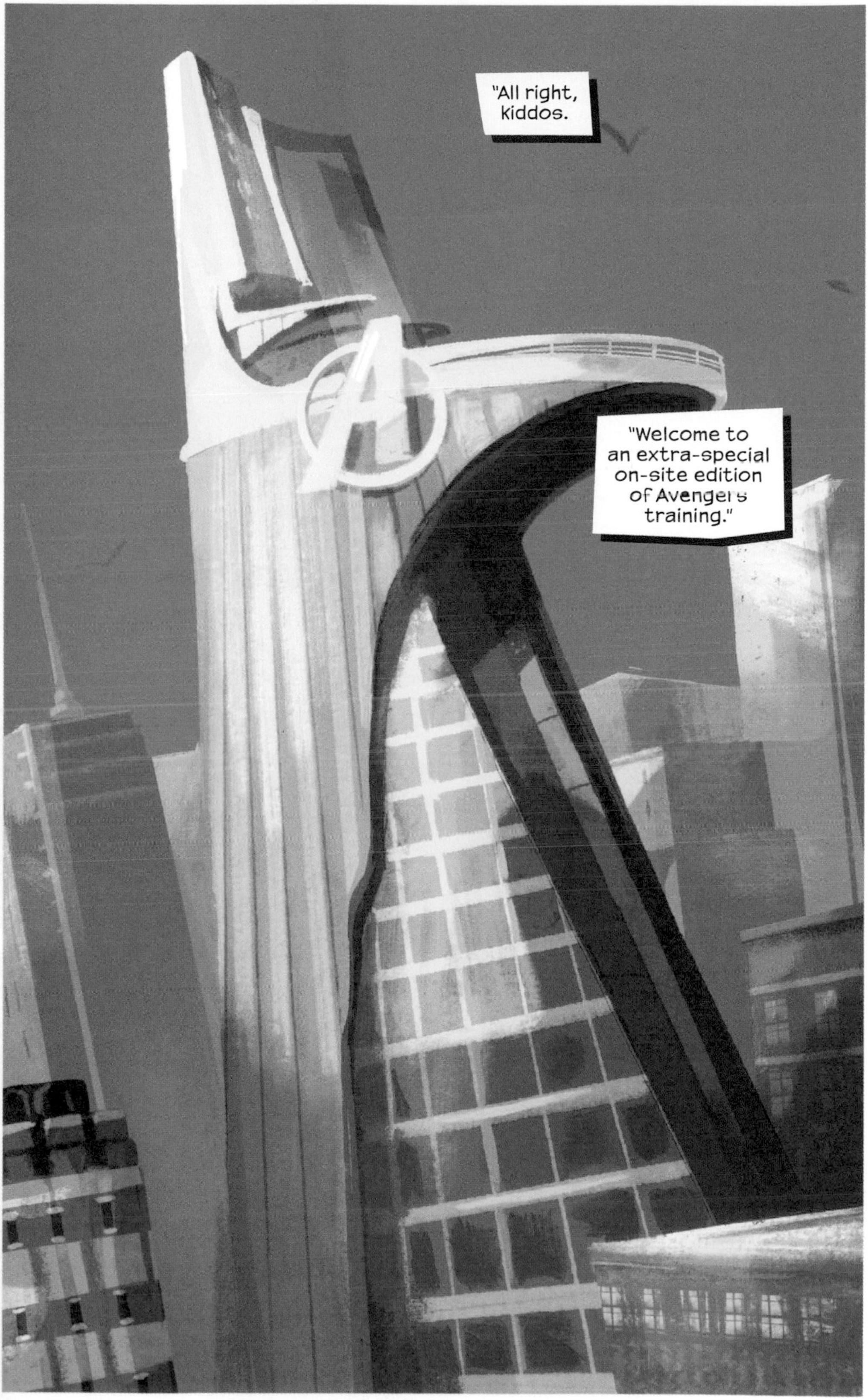
"All right, kiddos.
"Welcome to an extra-special on-site edition of Avengers training."

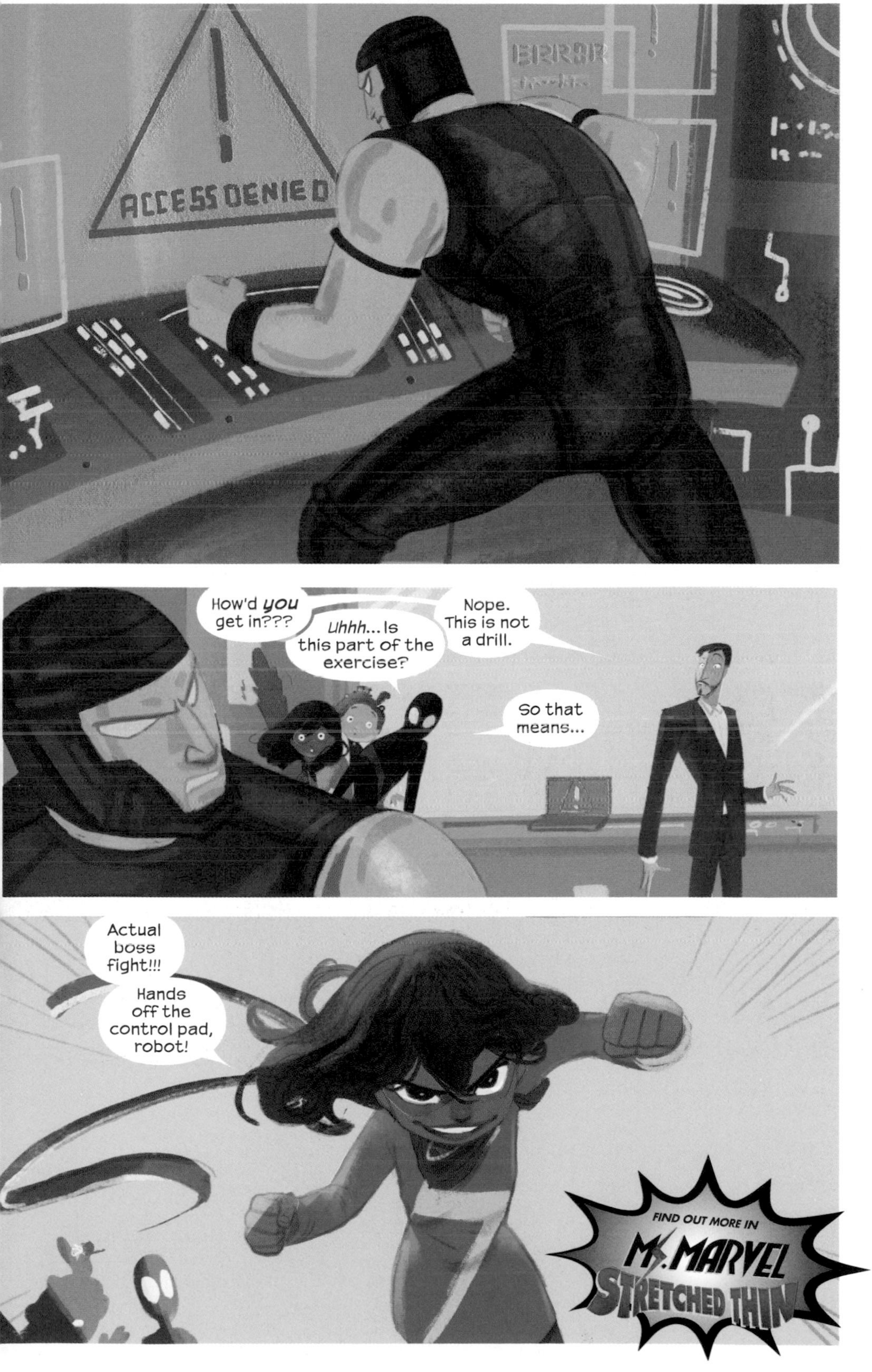
ACCESS DENIED
ERROR
How'd *you* get in???
Uhhh... Is this part of the exercise?
Nope. This is not a drill.
So that means...
Actual boss fight!!!
Hands off the control pad, robot!
FIND OUT MORE IN
MS. MARVEL
STRETCHED THIN